The Merlin Manuscript

Jan McDonald

Raven Crest Books

Copyright © 2014 Jan McDonald

The right of Jan McDonald to be identified as the author of this work has been asserted by her in accordance with the Copyright, Designs and Patents Act 1988

ISBN-13: 978-0-9929387-2-7
ISBN-10: 0-99-293872-4

"And so, perhaps, the truth winds somewhere between the road to Glastonbury, Isle of the Priests, and the road to Avalon, lost forever in the mists of the Summer Sea."

The Mists of Avalon – Marion Zimmer Bradley

PROLOGUE

The Once and Future King lay dying. Only Avalon could save him now.

Bedevere, known in his home country of Wales as Bedwr, stood at the water's edge, his heart keeping time with the rhythmic lapping of the water at his feet. The sword in his hand was too great a treasure, too great a responsibility and too great a destiny to be borne by one man alone. And yet, to destroy it would take away nothing of its burden. To throw it into the lake felt like blasphemy.

He closed his eyes and drew a breath. Twice he had failed in the task set him. Twice he could not throw the sword. Now, thrice he had failed.

Each time he had returned to the dying king, his failure had been written on his face, his secret known. He asked for a vision, and it was granted.

He closed his eyes, and in his vision he saw the sword leave his hand in a great arc, and descend upon its path towards the still grey water of the lake.

A blinding light surrounded it, and a slender hand emerged from the cold, dark depths of the lake to grasp the sword by its golden hilt. For a moment, the world was stilled. For a moment, time and destiny had no meaning. There was only the sword in the light.

Bedwr opened his eyes to the falling twilight, and took his own destiny by the hilt.

With a deep intake of breath, he raised the sword high above his head. He let out a cry that was heard in the Otherworld as he drove the sword into the ground, where it stood before him; firm in his failure; locked in his betrayal; and where he would return later to reclaim it.

Excalibur and the destiny of Britain were entwined

upon another day.

He returned to Arthur, who lay between life and death, and answered him.

'Sire, the sword is thrown into the lake. A great light surrounded it, and a hand that surely belonged to a woman of such beauty that I was not worthy to gaze upon her countenance, grasped it from the air. She has taken the sword to the bosom of the lake."

The king thus satisfied, rested and awaited the silent barge that would come from the mist to carry him back to Avalon from whence he came, where his Great Rest awaited him.

On a nearby hillside known as Brighid's Mound, that was the western gateway to Avalon, an old man raised his head; white-haired, white-bearded, wisdom in every pore. He heard the cry of betrayal in his heart. Excalibur was lost.

Britain was lost.

Lost to the God of the Romans and the invading Saxons. The Goddess saw it, and she wept. Her tears were copious and her grief immense, but her tears were not for herself for She was Eternal; she shed them for her children, and the persecution and bloodshed that they would suffer, forced into abandonment of the Old Religion by the Roman Church. Their ways were ways of masculine force and separation from the land; her ways were ways of love and unity with the land, where her children came to her willingly, with love, and without coercion. Now they were lost to a world where avarice and materialism were becoming the new Gods. And one day her children would return to her by the heart, and not the sword.

And she wept.

Then through Her veil of tears she saw it. A day would dawn when her children would rise again and say 'Enough!', and she saw a girl child, an infant who would become the Lady of Avalon, and unite the two worlds again; a child born in the outer world but with the heart of Avalon in her soul. She looked upon the child in the sweetness of her innocence, and she gave her a gift. A gift bestowed from the Goddess herself, which would shine a light in the barren land of the outer world.

And he, Merlin, would see a day far distant, when the fate of both lay in his own gnarled hands once again. All he could do now was to set the events on parchment alongside one of his gravest prophecies, for another hand to find at some future day of need.

From his satchel formed from wolf skin, he drew a parchment on which he had written his last prophecy. He returned his hand to the satchel and took out a goose feather that he had fashioned into an instrument of writing. A glass vial followed, containing ink that he had made from charcoal and herbs.

Beneath the prophecy he set his words.

And now, ten years on, his enemy was upon him.

He looked down at the sword at his feet, the sword he had wrenched from the dying hand of Rhydderch Hael to whom it had passed from Bedwr, and made a decision that would resonate into the distant future.

He picked up Excalibur, raised his hands to the heavens and closed his eyes. The words of the spell rang from his lips, as he cast the sword forever into the heart of Avalon; into the heart of what would become known as Glastonbury Tor. There it would be safe where only he, or the Pendragon, would be able to retrieve it - but the last Pendragon lay sleeping in time, until the country had need of him again. Excalibur must leave the world too, and wait for that day.

A scream of anger rent the air; and she stood before him then, tall and elegant, cream-skinned and beautiful with her finely etched features of the faerie folk, her hair an auburn halo. She was his love, his lust, his passion - and his obsession. Nimue.

Death was in her bright green eyes, his death. He had

3

seen it long ago in a vision, his death at the hand of his love. And now she had come for him.

Some knew her as the Lady of the Lake, generous and giving. Others knew her dark side; the wrathful, power-hungry sorceress - a gift which he had himself bestowed upon her, as he surrendered all warnings and omens of treachery, sharing all of his magickal knowledge with her. Now she was his equal. And now she wanted rid of him.

"Merlin, did you really believe there was a place in this world that I would not find you?"

"What is it that you want of me, Nimue? You have the last of my magick; I have nothing else to give to you."

"I want you gone."

She read his instincts in a moment in time; and her arm flew out in front of her, her finger pointing at him, directing her power to contain him in a vortex of energy that even he could not break through. A force that ripped through the veil, sending Merlin to Brighid's Mound in the outer world.

"This mound shall be your tomb, Merlin. My friend, my lover, my teacher," she whispered. "Avalon shall not have you." The ground trembled; and a chasm opened into a deep cavern, where she cast him. With a deep rumble from beneath her feet, the entrance to the cave closed behind him. A tear formed at the corner of her eye and fell silently onto the ground that concealed the entrance to his cave. "This shall be your eternal home. Farewell, Merlin of Britain."

Bereft, and grieving at her treachery, he threw out his protection; his own power encompassing him in the light of truth and magic. Taking him from this world into another. Beyond that light was only darkness, as the crystals grew around him. Tall and clear as water, their points reaching heavenwards, the crystals grew. He felt their magic, their protection, their energy; and one crystal that glinted in the darkness more than the others, encompassed him, sealing him inside its own heart. His crystal coffin.

And so Merlin faded into history, leaving only the enigma of his being, and an old satchel fashioned from wolf skin. Faded into a cave of crystal within the mound sacred to the Goddess Brighid, not dead but asleep, waiting for the time when Britain will have need of him again. When his prophecies would come into being.

And there he slept, until one day....

CHAPTER ONE: BORN DIFFERENT

Mike Travis stood looking out of his study window over the garden of their black-and-white Tudor cottage that ran down to the Mill Brook; the cottage in rural Monmouth that they had lived in for just over two years, and at the persistent rain that had soaked them and lowered their spirits day upon day. The telephone was cradled against his ear as he listened to his friend Jack's agitation.

His thoughts wandered briefly over their time together. Jack Carter was his best friend. They had been comrades at first, both posted into the same RAF squadron after their pilot training, and then serving together in war-torn Afghanistan. Then, when Mike had been shot down, Jack had sat by his bedside waiting for the coma to lift, willing it to do so. Waiting for him to live - willing him to recover. And when Mike had pulled through, with enough metal in his leg, as he put it, to start a scrap metal business, and a livid scar that ran the length of his cheekbone, Jack was there throughout his recovery, had believed in him when Mike had discovered that he had returned from death with a strange gift; a gift that enabled him to see into the Otherworld. He could sense and see spirits. And other things. Things that were best unseen.

Since then, Jack had fallen victim to savage government cuts that had decimated the Armed Forces to less than essentials. He'd taken his redundancy pay-out and expertise, and started his own helicopter charter business out of Cardiff airport. They had stood together as civilians, facing spiritual evil together, and beating it. Jack was godfather to his two-year-old daughter, Adain, who was as much a part of their lives as the air they breathed, and his wife, Beth, loved Jack as much as he did.

Jack's voice brought him back from the brief reverie. ".... and it's not what Ben thought it was. Originally he believed it to be a run-of-the-mill treatise on black magick. You know, old grimoire, all that kind of stuff. But it isn't. It's more than that, much more. You should come and see for yourself, Mike. It's important."

Eighteen months had passed since they had faced the demon Ahriman; blissfully quiet months, when they had all passed their time in normal everyday life. Eighteen months since Ben had recovered the old documents from Rhydderch Manor, but had only recently begun to translate the Latin text.

Now, as he listened to his friend, he sensed that peace was about to become history.

" ... Mike, are you there?"

"Yep. I'm listening." But he was distracted; something wasn't right, something was different that morning.

He'd sensed it when he was in the shower; even the water seemed to have an unnatural stillness about it. The mist over the garden was slow to lift and the damp morning air seemed to have an echo to it. It felt as if he was standing between two worlds.

And he knew in his gut that it meant something bad was coming.

Beth's even but insistent voice came from the sitting-room. "Mike, come here. Now."

Her tone told him that now, meant now. "Jack, I'll call you back."

"Sure. Everything OK?"

He frowned. "Not sure." He disconnected the call.

Beth was standing in the sitting room doorway, a frown of concern lining her brow. He followed her eyes to their daughter sitting on the rug in the centre of the room. Adain was chuckling gleefully, her brilliant sapphire eyes dancing with delight as she played with a small teddy bear that had been a present from Jack. It was her favourite toy which she took with her everywhere. Now she was giggling

8

heartily, as it twirled and somersaulted in the air above her.

Mike's heart missed a beat at what he was seeing.

Adain's chubby little fingers were pointing towards the airborne teddy, and as she wriggled them, the bear tumbled and danced in the air, causing her to chuckle even more deeply.

He put his arm around Beth. They had watched Adain carefully, watching and waiting for something like this, watching the intelligence developing too fast behind those distinctive eyes. Eyes that Mike had seen in another child. Grace. His friend Josh Hammond's daughter.

Since he had made the connection, he had read exhaustively about what had become known as the Indigo, and the Crystal Children; children born with a vastly-developed awareness of their earthly home; born to bring peace and greater spiritual understanding to their world. Born different.

'Gifted' didn't come close.

He thought about Grace. She had been diagnosed with severe autism; locked in her own world, not speaking, not interacting with any other human being for all of her six years - not even her mother. Until the day she had stood with Mike in a cave in the Sinai desert, and activated the lost Ark of the Covenant. She had spoken for the first time that day. It seemed like a lifetime ago. Grace, with her equally dazzling eyes.

Mike saw those eyes echoed in his daughter's. He stared down at her, his heart full of something like pride, tinged with fear. The day they had watched for had arrived.

He pulled Beth to him and squeezed her. The time for speculation was over, Adain's life was going to be vastly different; and they knew that it would be full of challenges. Challenges that they would meet head on, protecting her whilst allowing her the space to develop whatever gifts that were coming her way.

Beth bent to pick up Adain. The child turned her attention to her mother, and the teddy bear fell onto the rug.

Adain looked up at them and chuckled happily. "Can I have juice please Mummy?"

Beth and Mike exchanged looks of anxiety, but they fought to stay calm at their daughter's words, words that shouldn't be a part of her vocabulary for some time yet. She planted a kiss on the tousled head and walked into the kitchen in a daze, with Adain toddling happily behind her.

The telephone rang, and the screen on the phone told Mike it was Jack calling again. He answered it. "Jack. Look, something's come up, I can't talk right now."

There was a silence at the other end and then Benjamin Lovecraft's deep voice filled his head.

"It's Ben, Mike. Something's happened. They've got Jack."

Mike took several moments to process the thought. "What did you say?"

"They've taken Jack. I think he's hurt, Mike."

If there had been any fragment of sanity left in his day, it just went south.

"I'm coming over."

CHAPTER TWO: HERESY

TWO DAYS EARLIER - THE PALACE OF THE HOLY OFFICE, ROME

The Prefect read the newspaper article in silence - and then slammed it down onto his desk in fury, staring over the top of his spectacles, his eyes alight with fire. The fire of deep-seated fanaticism that would burn for an eternity, fuelled constantly by the heretical world outside his walls; walls that enclosed the Holy Office, otherwise known as The Congregation for the Doctrine of Faith, and previously known by its more infamous title – The Inquisition.

Monsignor Paolo Orletti took an involuntary step back; such was the malice that spewed forth from the Archbishop. "*Why am I only seeing this now?* This article is *eighteen* months old!" barked the Archbishop. "Who do we have over there?"

Orletti felt sick. He was permanently of a nervous disposition and clearly unsuited to his role within the Inquisition. He was a round man, with huge round spectacles which sat on a small beaky nose, giving the impression of a panicky owl.

The Prefect was clearly looking for someone to take a hit for this perceived negligence, being as hard and ruthless on his staff as he was on the heretics. His appointment had been a surprise and a concern to many conservative Catholics, as his belligerence and authoritarian attitude already engendered comments and comparisons to the earlier name for the Congregation, that of 'The Inquisition'. He didn't care about the comments. God had granted him the privilege of rooting out such evil, and he would do whatever it took to accomplish it, above and beyond any papal guidelines. It was his calling, his honour and duty, to root out and eradicate all heresy *and* its perpetrators. A divine calling that he had worked long and hard for, and he wasn't about to let this slip through his fingers. No. That would never happen. Especially this one. The Holy Office had gone soft. It was pain and suffering would bring souls back to the fold, not pandering to modernism.

Renegade priest and exorcist, Father Benjamin Lovecraft had walked away from the Church, defrocked and excommunicated for disobedience and distortion of the Church's law. If the Prefect had had his way, Lovecraft would still be rotting in one of the dungeons under the Vatican itself. Heresy was intolerable enough, but heresy from a priest was an abomination.

He stared down at the newspaper as if it would give him the answers he sought. The headline alone was enough to ring alarm bells, and yet it had taken all this time to arrive on his desk.

Rhydderch Manor, in rural Monmouthshire, had suffered massive structural damage during a freak earthquake, the epicentre of which was directly underneath its medieval foundations. According to the report, Rhydderch Manor had recently been converted into a private psychiatric clinic, and housed several residential patients who had been rescued by three passers-by, ex-Catholic priest Benjamin Lovecraft, Mike Travis and Jack Carter. All patients were safely accounted for, although, sadly, Dr Stephen Samael and Charge Nurse David Monroe had perished in the collapse. The quake appeared to be localised, and there were no reports of further damage.

The name of Rhydderch Manor, coupled with Benjamin Lovecraft, could be no co-incidence. Rhydderch Manor had been gifted to Sir Robert Fitzalan back in the late eleventh century. Fitzalan had evaded the Inquisition and had carried out the most evil perversions, worshipping the Devil and all his foul works from the relative safety of the Manor. The Prefect knew this because he had made it his business to read the document relating to the matter, now safely housed in the Vatican Secret Archives. And the name 'Rhydderch' had appeared several times in other works linked with the most pernicious of heresies; those of the so-called magician Merlin, a sorcerer most cunning, who defended the pagans and barbarians of Britain in the sixth century, allying himself irrevocably with that hotbed of evil, the Isle of Avalon. Even the name made his stomach twist violently, threatening to eject his breakfast. Merlin, whose ravings and so called prophecies had kept the Old Religion alive - albeit driven underground by his esteemed predecessors, had spoken of the northern ruler Rhydderch Hael in context of another abomination; one which he would eradicate from the face of the earth if its existence was proven. A sword of sorcery known as Excalibur.

Because not to do so, could bring the entire edifice of the Church tumbling down over all Rome and the wider world.

His mind wandered to the book, dated 1474, Merlini Prophetica, housed in the Vatican library, among many thousands of books which are forbidden to be read by any other than the highest echelons of the Vatican. It sat alongside another, one that had never been heard of outside the closest papal circle, which was listed in The Index of Forbidden Books, and again contained prophecies and warnings that had in fact come to pass. Those he could do nothing about, but the others, well, there was no way on God's Earth that he would let those come to be. The book was entitled The White Book of Rhydderch, and although this work was widely known and documented, being in two parts, and containing mostly Welsh folklore, this copy contained a third part that had never been acknowledged. And this third part had been

13

credited to Merlin. At the end of the document was a note that hinted at another copy being in the possession of Sir Robert Fitzalan, inheritor of Rhydderch Manor.

He appeared to make a swift decision and Monsignor Orletti almost fainted with relief when he said in clipped tones, "I shall deal with this myself. Make the appropriate travel arrangements". But Orletti's relief was short lived, as the Prefect pinned him with his cold black eyes and added. "For two. And arrange to connect with our UK operatives."

The Monsignor was only too pleased to make his escape, but his relief was tinged with foreboding that this wasn't going to end well for someone. The Prefect had a look of black determination set around his hard mouth and cold eyes.

Alone in his office, the Prefect locked his door and crossed to a large cabinet against the far wall. His breathing was deep and heavy, as he prepared himself for his ritual. He opened the cabinet with reverence.

Inside the cabinet was what could only be described as a shrine. A large ornate cross stood centre stage, and laid out before it was the ritual scourge that was to be the instrument of his voluntary penance. Pain as an offering had long been a part of him.

He removed his upper clothing and stood bare-chested, as he picked up the scourge slowly and put it to his lips. The wooden handle terminated in knotted leather thongs, on the ends of which were small pieces of jagged bone and metal balls which would serve as the device of his atonement. Atonement for past deeds, and for his actions that were soon to become reality.

His back bore the many scars of previous flagellation, criss-crossing his torso in a livid reminder of his entrenched belief that suffering was the only way to penitence. Whatever heinous acts he was about to commit would be vindicated by the result: more heretics would obey or die.

He began to intone the prayer.

The first lash on his back brought a red weal diagonally from his shoulder blade to his waist. He didn't flinch. The second was harder, and the jagged bone bit into his flesh. There was a flicker of a smile as he felt himself submitting to his punishment. After the third lash, the flagellation took up a steady rhythm, cutting and bruising his body as he gritted his teeth against the pain of the lacerations. His back was covered in blood and fresh bruising was appearing on top of the yellow signs of previous healing.

His mind journeyed back to his childhood. He was thankful for this shift, because it took him to a place where the lesson of suffering had first been beaten into his consciousness.

His father was a fanatical Catholic of the old school, attending Mass that was said in Latin and despising what he saw as heresy - the demand for Mass in modern Italian. He beat his son regularly, especially when he hadn't transgressed, and when that son turned fifteen he introduced him to the ritual act of self-flagellation. It had become a comfort to the Prefect during the long cold hours in his room, where he was locked for long periods of time to study. The seminary was the only place for him.

Just after his sixteenth birthday he had been shocked and disgusted when, in his father's absence, he had discovered his mother in front of what he could only understand as the Devil's altar. She was in the garden, kneeling before a stone seat. It had been draped in white satin and, at first glance, there was a statue of the Holy Virgin in the centre. His mother had lit a candle and appeared to be deep in devotion, so much so that she was unaware of his presence. As he stole silently closer, he was appalled to see that it was not in fact, the Holy Virgin, but a statue of the Italian pagan Goddess Aradia, the Goddess of the Moon.

His gasp of horror brought his mother to her feet. When she saw the look of hatred and disgust on his face she flung herself at him, crying and pleading with him not to tell his father. Pleas that found no answering compassion. He pushed her away from him violently, with cries of 'Strega!' '*Witch!*'

He lost no time in reporting the incident to his father on his return, and was unsurprised and unmoved by the sight of his mother later that day, bearing the marks of being shown the error of her ways. He showed no emotion the following day when enquiring as to her whereabouts, he was told that she had remained unrepentant and had left the house. He never saw her again.

He replaced the scourge before the cross, and asked for a blessing on his mission. He then took a towel from one of the drawers beneath the shrine and did his best to clean up his back before replacing his shirt. He bowed his head and locked the cupboard again. The next time he opened it would be to remove the scourge and pack it in his suitcase.

CHAPTER THREE: THE INQUISITION

Mike followed Beth into the kitchen. Adain was sitting happily at her mother's feet, drinking apple juice.

Beth looked up at him, and her immediate concerns for their daughter slipped away as she looked at Mike's furrowed and pale face.

"Who was that?" she asked.

"Ben," he said. "He kept saying that someone had taken Jack, and that he thought he was hurt. I'm sorry but I need to go over there, love." He looked meaningfully at Adain.

Beth nodded vigorously, another layer of concern etching her own elfin features. "Yes. Go," she said, almost pushing him towards the door. "And call me."

Mike dropped a kiss on her lips, and bent to treat Adain to the same. Then he was out of the door.

Ben's cottage was in the centre of a small wood just outside the village boundary of Skenfrith. Driving past the ruins of the castle, Mike raised a hand in acknowledgement to the figure in the round tower, said to be the ghost of a Lady-in-waiting from Tudor times who had been killed by her lover. Sometimes he saw her at the top of the round tower, sometimes walking around the perimeter wall. She didn't respond.

Minutes later, he stopped his car in a small gravelled area at the side of the lane. There was no access for a vehicle to Ben's cottage, and Jack's car was already parked in the pull-in. Mike parked behind Jack's red Audi, unhooked the chain on the gate and hurried through the woods to the cottage.

The door stood open and the cottage was silent, emphasised by the absence of the noisy greeting that usually came from Fred, Ben's Rottweiler. He knocked on the open door and stepped inside.

His immediate impression was one of a hurricane having gone straight through the cottage. Ben's books were strewn everywhere, furniture was upturned, and there were files and papers scattered across the quarry tiles. Ben was sitting at the table smoking one of his roll-ups. Instead of the usual steaming teapot in front of him, there was a half empty bottle of brandy.

Mike stared at Ben. He looked smaller than usual, diminished somehow. The huge bear of a man had been brought low.

Two strides took Mike across the room. He put his hand on Ben's shoulder. "Ben?" His voice faltered as he took in the sight of Fred, lying on the floor at his feet, panting hard and giving the occasional whimper. Mike bent over the dog and stroked his ear. Fred opened a bloodshot eye, seemed to settle, and closed it again.

Mike looked back up at Ben; he hadn't appeared to move and there was ash growing from the end of his roll up.

"*Ben!* What the hell...?

Ben took a drag from his cigarette and blew out the bluish smoke in a long drawn-out exhalation. He swallowed hard, as he looked down at the sorrowful Rottweiler. "They knocked Fred out cold and shut him in the cupboard under the stairs. Then they did all this." He gestured around the room with his hand. "And they've taken Jack."

Mike frowned. "Who? Who are *they*? *Where the hell is Jack?*"

Ben grimaced. "They call themselves the 'Congregation for the Doctrine of Faith'. You probably are more familiar with their old name, Mike. The Inquisition."

Mike's eyes narrowed, "The *what?* Ben what's this all about? I only spoke to Jack less than an hour ago. He was here, and he was fine - a bit agitated, but I didn't think there was anything seriously wrong. His car is still in the lane."

Ben nodded and pointed to the floor. Mike followed his fingertip to the fireside rug. He felt himself go pale as he bent down to gingerly touched the large, dark stain on the rug, and brought his finger away red with blood. He swallowed hard, and looked down again at the fitfully sleeping dog.

Ben shook his head again, "He's OK; feeling sorry for himself, that's all, poor sod." He took another drag. "That's not Fred's blood, Mike"

Mike sat down heavily, facing Ben. "Tell me what this is about, Ben. Jack called me earlier, but I had to leave the conversation. That was barely an hour ago."

Ben nodded, "I was over with Dai Bricks. I'd nearly finished with the translation. It *was* the third part to the White Book of Rhydderch, but it's not what I first thought."

"Yep, Jack said something like that."

"It took me a long while to translate it all. The Latin was easy, but the last part of it was in a mixture of Old Welsh and some form of runic script. The Old Welsh was proving tricky; it's probably the only text in the original Celtic that's been seen for a very long time. Dai was giving me a hand with it. I had to be really careful, handling it as little as possible; it's very fragile. I made copies of every page so that I could work more easily."

Mike was impatient. "Get to the point, Ben! What's this got to do with Jack?" he demanded.

"Once I realised what I was dealing with, I was even more careful. I only told Jack and Dai because I had a hunch that if it was real, then the less people that knew about it the better. I needed Dai's help with the Old Welsh and Jack, well, you know Jack, I had to tell him in the end. He can be very persistent."

Mike sighed, "So, are you going to tell me what's in the manuscript or not?"

"It's known as the Merlin Manuscript. Consisting of a lot of his prophecies and magic spells, just as you'd expect, but at the end were some very specific instructions. It gives the whereabouts of Excalibur.""

Mike stood up abruptly and ran his fingers through his hair. He didn't speak for several minutes.

"OK, listen. I'm not going to discuss magic swords with you right now, we need to find Jack."

"If we wait a bit longer, we will", said Ben. He pulled a crumpled piece of paper from his pocket, and tossed it across the table.

Mike picked it up and smoothed it out. "Where did this come from?" he said quietly.

"Jack's phone was on the table. I used it to call you. The note was wrapped around it."

Mike hadn't given a thought to the fact that Ben had called him from Jack's phone. He frowned, and turned his attention back to the note.

The letters were exquisitely written - painstakingly so - in precise copperplate and in ink. "You will be contacted at twelve o'clock with instructions. Call the police and he WILL die." Mike looked at his watch; it was eleven thirty.

"What are you saying? Jack's been kidnapped? Why? They won't get much of a bloody ransom! Talk to me Ben, you aren't serious about the Inquisition?"

"I'm afraid I am, Mike. They're watching brief is to uphold and spread the doctrines of the Church, and to stamp out heresy wherever they see it. However they see it. This manuscript? The original is in the Vatican Library, safe under lock and key and away from unauthorised eyes. This is a later copy, and one that no-one thought existed. They'll do anything to stop it becoming public property. In fact I can't think of anything that they won't do to get it. Jack was in the wrong place at the wrong time. I have no idea how they knew it was here. It's the manuscript they wanted, and it wasn't here." He thumped on the table and his glass nearly went over. "And neither was I," he growled.

Ben reached out for the brandy, but Mike grabbed his wrist. There was a brief flash of warning from Ben, but it subsided quickly and he let his hand fall back onto the table.

Mike's head was in turmoil, and he was more abrupt than he'd meant to be. "You can sit here and get pissed if you want. But I'm going to find Jack! And in the thirty minutes that's left you're going to give me a history lesson. Tell me everything. For a start, how did you know about this ... manuscript?"

"Just before I was appointed as an exorcist, I did a short stint in Rome. I shared rooms with Father Dominic Royce; he was a taciturn Irishman of very few words, but we got on. His post was Assistant to the Archivist in the Vatican Secret Archives. Nic - Father Royce - had a problem. He couldn't stay away from the single malt. Too much single malt. And one night he didn't come home when he should have. It wasn't unusual, and wouldn't normally have caused a problem, except that night one of the senior Cardinals, Cardinal Rafael Cardoni, was looking for him. I knew where he used to hide out with his bottle, so I went to try and find him." He paused thoughtfully, reliving that night.

Mike frowned but said nothing, sensing that Ben was slowly coming to the point and wouldn't be pushed.

Ben continued. "The Archives are next to the Vatican Library, and the entrance is through the Porta di Santa Anna on the Via Porta Angelica, spitting distance from our lodgings. Entrance is restricted by digital code and swipe card, but I knew where he kept his duplicate card. He'd lost the original on a bender one night, and it turned up later inside his underpants! Didn't ask!" he gave a harsh laugh, "And I also knew his code; he was extremely vocal when he was pissed. So, I went in to give him the heads up that the Cardinal was on the warpath, hoping to give him time to at least get himself together, if not to sober up a little. Nic worked in the new underground facility, and he used to take his bottle into the Index Room where there was a small annexe attached, no more than a large cupboard really. Anyway, that's where I found him. Alive, but unconscious, and he'd taken more than just a bottle in there that night; he had Merlin's manuscript. I had to think quickly. I couldn't be found there, but I had to help him. I put him in the recovery position and pressed the alarm bell. It was then he regained consciousness briefly. He looked at me and said, 'Find Paradise'. That's all, just 'Find Paradise', and then he passed out again.

"I couldn't let him be found with the manuscript either, so I took it from him and put it on the Archivist's desk, among a load of other documents in the main room. But I'd already got a good look at what Nic was holding on to. Then I got out of there and watched. It only took a couple of minutes for the response to the alarm. Cardinals and the Swiss Guard were swarming all over the place in minutes, and immediately after that an ambulance turned up. That's when I went back to our rooms. A few hours later, Cardinal Cardoni himself turned up and told me that Nic was dead. He'd got drunk and choked on his own vomit, he said. Well, I knew that was a lie. I'd seen to him myself, put him in a position where that couldn't happen, and in any case, help arrived so quickly ... and it was odd that a senior Cardinal would come to tell me that. He insisted that I go with him - to pray for Nic, he said; I had no choice. And, when I eventually got back to our rooms, I could tell someone had been there. Nothing was obviously out of place, but when you have little in the way of possessions you know when they've been moved. Something wasn't right.

"I thought about what Nic had said. It sounded as if he knew he was dying, but it didn't fit; the guy regularly drank himself into oblivion. Then I remembered. He had an antique copy of Milton's 'Paradise Lost', was that what he meant by 'Find Paradise'? It wasn't difficult to find; it was still on the bookshelf in his room. Inside the back cover written in Latin in tiny handwriting was a detailed account of the manuscript he'd been holding. I recognised the title. It detailed the whereabouts of another copy of the manuscript. It was in Rhydderch Manor, Mike. Inside Fitzalan's tomb."

Comprehension dawned immediately on Mike, and his pent up emotions of the morning spilled out. "*So that's what you bloody well risked your life for!* And Jack's!" he said, remembering the night when the Manor was collapsing around them but Ben had stayed too long in the rubble in the cellar, searching for the document, and then Jack had gone back into the falling masonry to help him.

"Well, I hope it was worth it!" Mike wanted to take back the bitterness in his voice as soon as the words were out, but it was too late: they had hit home. They both knew it was because of the manuscript that Jack was now in deep trouble.

Ben began to roll another cigarette. "The day after Nic died, I was given another assignment. I was sent back to London, to a run-down parish in a deprived area of the East End. They wanted to keep me out of the way, and too busy to think about things. But I kept Nic's book, and I never stopped thinking that, for whatever reason, they killed him. But that was too horrifying to contemplate. Soon after that I was appointed as an exorcist and you know what happened then. Afterwards, I came here to carry on with things in my own way, and only subconsciously did I think about Rhydderch Manor. But when you came to me about Victoria Little, and the Manor came into things, well, it seemed like destiny was giving me a shove."

"When were you going to tell me?" Mike asked, in a small voice that betrayed his feelings.

"When I knew exactly what I was dealing with – and, in any case, I was going to help you with Victoria regardless. If I hadn't had the opportunity to find the manuscript, I would have let it be."

Mike could see by Ben's face that he spoke the truth, and that he was as stricken by Jack's disappearance as he was. He put a hand on Ben's arm: "So, tell me what's in this bloody manuscript!"

CHAPTER FOUR: THE LADY OF AVALON

Beth stood in the kitchen: her hands were in the sink, washing dishes, but her mind was in another place. Images of Adain's possible future paraded themselves through her head like scenes from an old movie. She shook herself free of the imagery, but her anxiety-level only deepened. Outside the window, their cat was stalking some unwary prey through the grass. It matched her thoughts exactly. Something was coming towards them, and they weren't going to be able to stop it. And now this with Jack!

She shook the soapy water from her hands and dried them roughly.

"Don't worry, Mother. It will be all right." Adain's voice cut through everything else, finding its home in the dark recesses of her mind. *Mother*? What was that about? Addie had never called her that, nor - to her recollection - had even heard the word. At two, the child had always used the usual *Mummy*.

And deep in her core, she knew that Adain hadn't spoken at all.

She spun around to her daughter, who was sitting on the floor contentedly playing with her wooden blocks. Beth's sudden movement made her look up, and she beamed in her innocence at her mother.

Beth knelt on the rug and hugged her daughter. "Sweetheart, what did you say? ... Addie?"

For a moment Adain looked puzzled, and then she shook her head and returned to the pile of bricks. Beth hugged her again and began to pick up bricks randomly. "Shall we build a house?" she asked quietly, trying to keep the emotion from her voice.

Adain thrust her hand out in front of her and, as she did so, several of the larger bricks took to the air and flew across the room. The child's eyes darkened and her lip began to tremble, and she began to wail from the sheer and uncontrolled force of it. Beth grabbed her and hugged her tightly, her heart pounding in her chest, soothing her and stroking her hair.

She and Mike had known that Adain was different in some way. She had flown through all her infant milestones way ahead of the usual time and she was beautiful and healthy with a heightened intelligence behind those eyes that sometimes unnerved her. Although there had been nothing to alarm them unduly, her vocabulary was way ahead of her age - but it was those eyes that seemed to hold the wisdom of a thousand years, and their scary resemblance to Grace, that had kept them watching her closely. Now, they knew.

This was the beginning.

Beth looked up at the mantle clock: why hadn't Mike phoned her? He must have been at Ben's cottage by now. She picked up the telephone and frowned at it as if willing it to ring, then, quickly coming to decision, began to dial Jack's number.

Her fingers halted midway, as Adain pulled herself free of Beth's arms and wriggled to the floor, knocking over her tower of bricks as she did so. In a fraction of a moment her expression changed, and once again the wooden blocks were flying through the air. Beth gasped, but wasn't quick enough to dodge the one that hit her square on the forehead.

For a moment the room span, and there was a buzzing noise in her head. Then everything went dark. The last thing she was aware of was Adain's voice in her head, "*I'm sorry, Mother.*"

Beth fought to regain consciousness, reaching up through the darkness. She was standing in mist, or so it seemed, and everything was silent except for the sound of gently lapping water.

Then the sound changed, shifting ever so slightly, with the addition of the rhythmic sound of oars. She strained to see through the mist, and slowly, ever so slowly, it began to clear. She could just make out the water – and, as the mist cleared, everything seemed to be shimmering. Like heat on tarmac.

She cast her eyes heavenwards, and through the mist ahead of her, a tall conical hill was visible. Glastonbury Tor.

The rhythm of the oars didn't drop a beat, and as the mist cleared completely, she could see the long slender barge coming towards her. A young girl was pulling the oars, and at the prow was a striking, elderly woman. She had a black woollen shawl draped over her head, and pulled closely around her. Her eyes were sharp as gimlets, and there was an air of serenity about her that instantly calmed Beth.

The young girl turned to face her, and Beth felt the air leave her in a startled gasp. Olive skin and elfin features broke into a smile. The girl didn't speak, but Beth couldn't take her own gaze away from the face that held a haunting familiarity. The girl jumped lithely from the barge and pulled it in to the shore, steadying it for the old woman to disembark. She approached Beth slowly, allowing the shawl to fall across her shoulders.

Her snow white hair was coiled attractively around her head, and her beauty was unmarred by the obvious advanced years. The girl walked behind her, her attitude deferential, and Beth was shaken by the familiarity of her face.

The old woman spoke. "Please child, don't be afraid. You are between waking and sleep, and although you are fighting to return to your world, the time you spend here with me will be but seconds in your own time." She held out her hand to Beth, who took it tentatively, confusion eddying around her head like the water in the centre of the mist. And try as she might, she couldn't tear her gaze away from the girl.

She appeared to be around fifteen. Her dark hair was tied loosely into the nape of her neck, falling down her back in a single, long plait. She wore a long green dress that enhanced her olive skin and her otherworldly features. It fell to her ankles, and at her throat was an iridescent moonstone. She evoked a yearning in Beth that she didn't understand.

Until the young girl spoke.

"Hello, Mother."

Tears welled in Beth's eyes. Was she dead? How was this possible?

The old woman squeezed her hand. "It's all right child. Yes, this is your daughter, Adain. There is much for you to know and to understand. I know that things are happening to her - frightening things - but you also know that she has special gifts. Just how special, you have yet to know and understand." She paused. "There are others like her - you know of one other."

Beth nodded dumbly.

"Do you know where you are, child? Do you know who I am?"

A light seemed to have settled around the old woman, and the serenity that had first been apparent, intensified.

Beth asked quietly, "Are you The Goddess?"

The old woman shook her head and smiled at her, as her face became illuminated with an ethereal inner light. "No, child. Although I do speak for her here. I am Morgan La Fey, the Lady of Avalon. I am also known as Morgana, or Morrigan; you may call me Morgana." She gave Beth a few seconds for the information to filter through. "I see your confusion, child. I have lived for what seems an eternity, the voice of The Goddess here in Avalon. But I am of the Faerie Folk, hence my name, which simply means Morgana of the Faeries; my mother was Igraine and my father was of the faerie realm, not Gorlois of Cornwall as people have come to believe. Our lifespan is great, and our bodies age at a much slower rate than humans, but even we have an ending. My time is drawing to a close, and I am very old and very tired now. Adain will be the next Lady of Avalon. She is here for training, to learn how to control her gifts and to use them in the service of The Goddess. It is her destiny to bring our worlds together again: to heal the fractures brought about by the aggression and avarice of your dimension, which parted Avalon from your world so long ago." Her face softened, "I see the fear in your eyes, and the pain in your heart, but it won't be a loss to you. You will have free access to her when she comes to us on her first moon flow, and during her training. You won't grieve for her, but stand proud in your gift to the world. And yours is the decision whether to allow it or not, until she is of age to make her own choice. For now, though, you must understand that her gifts are as frightening to her as the implications of them are to you. You must bring her here, and I will take her to the stone circle at the top of the Tor, and to the Holy Well, where her gifts will be hushed until such time as she comes to me for her training. One of our priestesses is on her way to bring you here: her name is Rowan. You will know her by the crystal she wears at her throat. It is the colour of a kingfisher's wing, with the light of a thousand diamonds at its heart. Your husband, too, has a destiny that will bring him back here, and already the tides are rising to meet him in that journey."

Tears welled in Beth's eyes at the enormity of what the old woman was saying to her - not because of the fear the words invoked, but because of the truth in them that reached her innermost soul. She looked at Adain standing proud behind the old woman, and her heart seemed to grow inside her until she feared it would burst through her ribs.

She held out a hand to her daughter. Adain moved forward silently, as she always would from that time forward, seeming to glide gracefully with the power of the Goddess growing inside her. She leaned forwards and kissed Beth gently on the cheek. "It will be all right, Mother. You'll see." She beamed at her mother, and Beth was instantly infused with her serenity.

Beth smiled at her daughter. "I love you," she said.

Morgana turned to Adain. "Wait at the barge for me, child. I must have a few moments with your mother." Adain nodded, and lowered her head respectfully, casting a last smile at Beth.

The old woman continued, "Avalon has waited a long time for her, and it will continue to wait until she is ready, and you are ready to allow it. I can wait too. But for now, I must ask this of you. School her in the old ways that you hold dear. Bring her to the love of The Goddess, and her ways. Celebrate the festivals, and allow her to feel the flow of energy that lies within the land. I know you have this in your heart, so it will be no heavy duty. We will school her in the healing and magical arts, and the knowledge of the herbs. I will have no difficulty in finding volunteers for the task. And she must also be aware of the ways of *your* world, for how else can she be instrumental in restoring harmony between the two?"

"But, surely, one of the other priestesses is more suitable to succeed you?" Beth whispered.

The old woman smiled. "Each of them knows their own destiny, and each destiny is as important to the whole as every other. They too have waited for your daughter. You will wake soon, and only a moment will have passed in your world. But remember this, you must bring her here. In Glastonbury lies the door and you will be given entry. Return now to your child, and know that you are blessed."

"What will happen if she doesn't wish it?"

Morgana looked over her shoulder, and Beth followed her eyes to the serene expression on her daughter's face. But what if she had a choice and she chose No? What of

Avalon then?

Morgana read her thoughts. "Then Avalon will fade forever into the mists;- no longer will there be any contact between the two worlds."

Beth tried to speak, but the feeling of displacement had returned. There was a sharp pain at her temple and she sat up too quickly. Adain sat in front of her still playing with her wooden blocks. She looked up at Beth and smiled at her; the same smile that she had seen on the lips of the beautiful fifteen-year-old in Avalon.

She gathered Adain into her arms hugging her tightly, and this time Adain didn't wriggle free. She nestled into Beth contentedly, and soon she fell asleep, blissfully unaware of what the future would hold for her, as she lay enfolded in her Mother's arms. A feeling so special, that the Welsh had given it a name. *Cwtch*.

Between the worlds on the edge of Avalon, another stirred. Nimue had slept there in silence, waiting for her revenge on Merlin and the Lady of Avalon. So, there was another who would wear the mantle of Avalon instead of her? Well, if she was not to be the Lady, then she would see to it that this usurper would be bent to her will. She would shape her, and make the child hers, and rule Avalon through her. Morgana would not have her way again. And if that failed, she would get rid of Morgana completely, and forever.

CHAPTER FIVE: FROM THE MANUSCRIPT

Mike glanced back at his watch. Fifteen minutes before the phone call. If there was going to *be* a phone call.

He was increasingly anxious, and the hollow feeling in the pit of his stomach emphasised his stress. What the hell was going on? Jack kidnapped, Adain displaying telekinetic abilities, Ben telling him that not only was the Inquisition alive and well, but it was baring its teeth in his face. He took a deep breath, and pulled his head back to the immediate.

He fixed Ben with a stare. "So? What is this all about? In as few words as possible."

"It's about the Catholic Church being afraid of people knowing the truth, Mike. You know what they say - spirituality is a connection with the divine, religion is crowd control. I know. I was part of it for too long. And I resent your assumption that you are the only one here that cares about Jack! I know that if it wasn't for me, he'd be safe right now. If I hadn't ..."

Mike saw the pain in Ben's eyes and backed off. "I'm sorry, Ben. Go on."

"There isn't time to tell you all of it. It's taken the best part of a year to decipher and decrypt it. Merlin was nothing, if not thorough. The prophecies were easy enough, being mostly in Latin. I mean, why write down prophecies that no-one can read, right? The magic spells were mostly written in Latin too, peppered with the odd runic script. Again, not so difficult. But the part that's in the old Welsh had me stumped for a while, until I sat down with Dai Bricks. And the reason for that was, that it turned out not to be old Welsh at all. Or at least, not completely. It was based on it, but some of the words seemed out of context, and when it was translated back it didn't make sense. Until we realised the old boy had used a code in it as well. Just a simple one that a school kid could crack, once we realised it *was* a code, but that was the clever part of it. And it's that part that's of interest to the Vatican. What do you know of the Arthurian legends, Mike?"

"I read Mallory's *'Morte D'Arthur'* in school, along with the mainstream legends. Why?"

"Do you believe that Arthur and Merlin were real historical characters?"

"Yes, actually."

"Good, then the rest of the manuscript will sit better with you. According to Thomas Mallory's epic poem about the death of Arthur, Sir Bedevere was the knight who eventually tossed the sword Excalibur back into the lake, yes?"

Mike nodded.

"Wrong. He didn't do it. He was granted a vision to relay to Arthur to make him believe that he had. But in fact, Bedevere, or Bedwr as he was known here in Wales, for whatever reason, betrayed Arthur, and hid the sword to reclaim later. Not only was this a betrayal of Arthur, but also of Nimue, the Lady of the Lake. It was she that granted the sword to Arthur, and on his death it was to be returned to her. It wasn't, and she was more than a tad pissed off about it. Excalibur was forged in Avalon by dragon fire, and was kept by the Lady of the Lake, and it was her prerogative to grant or withhold the sword. And she would only grant possession of the sword to the Pendragon."

Mike had begun pacing, impatient for Ben to get to the point. "What's this got to do with anything, interesting as it is?"

Ben sighed. "OK, ask yourself this. What would happen to the Church and its establishment if there was physical proof of magic, of the existence of Merlin – who, by the way, was also born of a virgin? What if the legitimacy of the Old Religion was proven, and the lies and deceits of the Vatican, which have absolutely nothing whatsoever to do with the teachings of the man from Nazareth, were exposed. What if you could hold Excalibur, what if you could bring forth Merlin from his crystal cave, bring Avalon back into the world? Don't you think that they would do anything to prevent that? The Old Religion is one of the fastest growing spiritual practices in this country, the United States, and the greater part of the western world, Mike. Fact. They call it 'Wicca' and have dressed it up in new fangled rituals, but at its core is the Old Religion; the religion of this country that was usurped back in the Dark Ages, when the New Religion was enforced by the sword on the people. What would happen to the money and the power of the Vatican then?

"I know you've been to Avalon. I know you've seen into the Otherworld. I know you've seen first-hand what they will do to retain the status quo. They were prepared to kill for possession of the Sacred Ark; don't you think they'll do the same for Excalibur? For Merlin?"

Mike frowned; his memories of being hunted by Vatican assassins were fresh in his head. He nodded his understanding. "I know," he said, "but would they really go to all that trouble for a sword? And who would believe that Merlin could still exist?"

"Mike, it's the sworn duty of the Inquisition to stamp out all heretical doctrines. And they don't care how they do it. They aren't going to allow validation of the Old Religion and magic, or sorcery, as they call it. Bloody hell, Mike, they killed their own pope because he was going to rock the Vatican boat. There are things in the manuscript ..." He was cut short by Jack's telephone ringing.

Ben's face was flushed with anger and alcohol as he made a grab for the phone. Mike got there before him, and hit the speaker button.

"Yes?" Ben snapped.

"You will come to the abandoned church of St. Mary the Virgin, just to the east of Tintern Abbey. Instructions of how to find it will be sent to you as soon as I disconnect this call. And you will bring the manuscript and *all* copies of it. I won't waste my breath telling you to come alone, as by now I expect Mr Travis is standing right next to you. No matter. You have one hour and a half. And in case you think to defy me, perhaps this may help."

A cry of agony came out of the speaker, and then *"Don't, Ben! Tell them to fuck off!"* Then another strangled cry and the phone went dead.

Ben was pale and visibly shaking. Mike shook his head; Jack never did know when to keep his mouth shut. His expression was grim and set, as he looked at his watch. One and a half hours was more than enough time to get to Tintern comfortably, if they left right away. An alert from Jack's phone told him that there was a text. He opened it and read the instructions.

He memorised them and put Jack's phone back onto the table with the note.

He turned to Ben, "Get everything you've got, and get in the car," he said quietly. Too quietly.

CHAPTER SIX: TO THE RUINED CHURCH

Mike looked at the bulging bag of papers in Ben's hand. "Is that everything? This is Jack's life on the line."

Ben's expression said that he was aware of the gravity of the situation. "Yes," was all he said.

Mike ran through the text from the Prefect in his head again, committing the instructions firmly to memory.

Come on foot from Tintern Abbey. Walk up to the A466, cross the road and proceed up the lane where the post box is located in a wall, until you reach a footpath beside a bungalow. Take the footpath, and you will reach the ruins. Inside the church you will find an opening in the floor, giving access to the crypt.

Once in the car Mike said, "So, tell me the rest. I can't believe that all this is because there's a document that gives the location of Arthur's sword, Excalibur."

"Obviously there was more to it. Merlin's prophecies are sometimes written in riddles, and sometimes his meaning is very plain. As I told you, contrary to common belief, Bedwr didn't return the sword to Nimue and she was mighty pissed and wanted it back.

"She was Merlin's lover and his apprentice - he gave her all of his knowledge and secrets - and she set out to kill him once she had everything from him. Merlin managed to stay alive because he had the power to dilute her spell, and instead of dying, he ended up trapped in a cave of crystal - not dead, not alive - just sleeping until someone reads the spell to release him.

"Also, because he threw out a blast of energy to protect himself, when Nimue's spell struck it, it rebounded on her like a boomerang. And, as she fell under her own spell, she too had the last word. She wouldn't die, but sleep, like Merlin.

"She had broken with Avalon prior to all this. Morgan Le Fey, or Morgana as some know her, the Lady of Avalon, was about to banish her because of her inflated sense of importance and blatant disregard for their ways. She challenged Morgana to the right to be the Lady of Avalon and lost, so there was no help for her from that quarter. As she fell asleep, she uttered a curse on Merlin's prophecy - that the next Lady of Avalon would be born in the land of the Cymru, born of a priestess of the Old Religion and a warrior. By the nature of her powers, she would need to be brought to Avalon as an infant, and the moment she was brought there, Nimue would take her revenge. She would wake from her long sleep and take the child for her own, and teach her the old ways in a twisted, polluted form. Gaining the power of Avalon for herself - but through the child."

Ben paused for Mike to assimilate all the information up to that point. He frowned as Mike obviously had yet to make the connection. He would have to give it to him in a simpler form.

"The next Lady of Avalon has distinctive eyes, Mike, and she will be imbued with telekinetic and telepathic powers." He waited for the penny to drop. It didn't. Or wouldn't.

"Adain is the next Lady of Avalon, Mike. She is named in Merlin's manuscript as Adain Le Fey, the Lady of Avalon."

Mike stepped on the brake too hard, and skidded to a sudden halt. He turned on Ben.

"What in God's name are you talking about? Addie? She has nothing to do with all this. Are you mental? And her name is Travis, Adain Travis."

"Le Fey simply means *of the Faerie folk,* but you know that. And I also know that you know, that the Faerie are not tiny winged creatures that sprinkle magic dust. It's the name given to the first inhabitants of this land, and to their descendants, some of who now live just beyond the veil and some on this side of it. It's all in there, Mike. Everything. And more."

"Hang on a minute. You said that Nimue blasted a spell at Merlin that was meant to kill him, but instead he ended up locked in a crystal cave, right?"

Ben nodded.

"Then how the hell could he have written about it in that bloody book?"

"He wrote all his prophecies from visions, Mike, long before that. He was a seer of extraordinary power. He wrote all this before his final meeting with Nimue; a meeting that he had seen in a vision too. It was probably why he was able to deflect her spell in time. He'd literally seen it coming."

Mike appeared to ponder on something, and so Ben stayed silent. Eventually, Mike said, "As far as my memory and limited knowledge of Merlin goes, he went mad. Yes?"

Ben nodded his agreement.

"So why would we be taking all this as fact, when it came from the mind of a madman?"

"After Arthur's death, Merlin became involved in many battles. It was in the Battle of Arfderydd that he saw his three brothers slaughtered. When he looked over the battlefield and saw all of the dead and dying, he fled the battle and lived in the forest, living as a wild man in a perpetual state of grieving. It was then he gained the title *Myrddin Wyllt* from the Cymru - *Merlin the Wild* in English. In this wild state, and living in nature, he began his prophesies."

Mike frowned, "My point exactly! He was obviously in the middle of some kind of breakdown, so why pay any heed to his ramblings?"

Ben smiled and began rolling a cigarette. "Because most of them have come true."

"You really set some store by all this?"

"Yes, Mike. I'm afraid I do."

"Well, Addie has nothing to do with this. You're wrong. She'll be involved over my dead body. You give these creeps that have Jack everything they want, you hear me? Everything." The tone in his voice brooked no dissention from Ben. Unlike Jack, Ben knew when to keep quiet.

After a few moments of intense silence, he said, "I would never do anything to hurt Jack. Or you, or Beth, or Addie. If you don't know that, then you don't know me."

Mike sighed. "I'm sorry. Of course I know that. It's just that I'd hoped that Addie would have a normal childhood, happy and carefree, with nothing in her future to blight her innocence. I've thought about leaving all this behind and doing something 'normal' for a living, but it doesn't seem to want to let me go. But I won't let anything come near her. Nothing. Especially now."

Ben let that comment go, and was quiet again before turning to Mike, "Then there is something else you should know. From what I can see, the part of the manuscript that talks about Adain and her connection to Avalon, talks of her as Lady Adain Le Fey, born in Wales in our world. If the Inquisition knows of this, they won't stop looking for her. She's as much a danger to them as Merlin himself. The good thing is, that it's either not in the manuscript they have, or, as yet, they haven't made that connection."

Mike ground his teeth, and caught the inside of his cheek as he bit down hard. He tasted his own blood and made a vow on it. "Then I'll make certain that doesn't happen."

He drove on for about half a mile and then said quietly. "Adain has telekinetic powers, Ben. This morning she levitated her teddy bear and was playing with it in mid-air, just using her mind and directing it through her fingers. Jesus, Ben, it was as natural to her as breathing."

"I think you have always known, deep down, that Addie was different; gifted in certain ways. Just like

Grace."

Mike looked sideways at Ben. He was about to say, 'What do you know about Grace?', when he realised that Jack must have told him everything, so he just nodded. He tried to put it out of his head. Adain was safe at home with Beth; it was Jack they had to concentrate on.

Thoughts of Jack made him frown. Although he wasn't a man of great physical stature, Jack had always been able to take care of himself. He'd never have gone willingly with the Inquisition and would have put up a fight, hence the blood on the carpet. He wondered what they had done to him, and winced as he heard again Jack's cry of agony.

It had been eighteen months ago that they had met Ben, and Mike had seen the change in his friend. He seemed happier and less erratic, quieter somehow. Mike decided to push the boundary of his friendship with Ben.

"Jack's very important to me, Ben. We've been through a lot together. In the Air Force, and since then. I wouldn't want to see him hurt. I think you understand me."

Ben nodded and smiled. "He'll take no hurt from me. You can depend on that."

Mike kept his attention on the road as they drove alongside the River Wye, as it meandered from Monmouth towards the village of Tintern. At any other time he would have appreciated the beautiful scenery along the English/Welsh border, but his mind was fixed on getting to Jack and doing as much damage to his captors as he could manage. And now he was in no doubt that the great bear of a man sitting beside him was equally ready for physical retribution.

They travelled the remainder of the journey in silence, each with his own demons, until, between the Wye and the road, the stone skeleton of the Cistercian Abbey reared up. Mike turned the car into a small lane just before the Abbey, and parked in the car park of the Anchor Inn, which was teeming with tourists.

Cross the road and proceed up the lane where the post

box is located in a wall until you reach a footpath beside a bungalow. Take the footpath and you will reach the ruins. Inside the church you will find an opening in the floor, giving access to the crypt. Bring the manuscript and all of your notes in exchange for your friend.

Directly across the road was an old stone wall in which there was a post box, next to a gothic doorway into the garden of the house elevated above them. The lane veered back on them like a hairpin, becoming a steep incline after only a few yards. Despite his size, Ben was very fit and was soon striding ahead of Mike.

The bungalow and its adjacent footpath came into view all of a sudden. And, after another steep climb, they found themselves looking at the ruined church of St Mary the Virgin, complete with ivy-clad tower and overgrown graveyard. The roof had long since passed into history, and even in daylight the ruined church spread its own atmosphere in tendrils towards them. Mike gave a passing thought to wonder how they had got Jack up there - oblivious to the fact that he was soon to wonder it again when he saw what else was in the crypt. He shook off the thought as irrelevant, and glanced down at his watch. They were there with fifteen minutes to spare.

They were both listening intently for sounds of people speaking, or worse. Everywhere there was silence as they picked their way through the overgrown graveyard and stepped inside the gothic arched doorway.

Inside the ruin there was a low murmur of voices and they rapidly spotted the large trapdoor in the middle of the floor. Ben approached it quickly and yanked on the handle. Light erupted from the crypt below as Mike moved up alongside Ben.

As they prepared to descend the ancient stone steps, Mike felt the stab of something hard and round in the middle of his back. It didn't take a fraction of a second to know that there was the barrel of a gun pushed against him, and that someone had stepped soundlessly out of the shadows behind them. He cursed violently at his own stupidity. He should have known there would be a welcoming committee, that served to act as guard as well.

Ben was simultaneously aware of the other presence, and stopped dead in his tracks also.

"Move," the man said, in a thick, sophisticated Italian accent. Rome, Mike thought.

He was suddenly pushed forward after Ben, and his titanium knee joint gave way, propelling him into his friend. Ben's bulk kept him from falling and he quickly steadied himself, even though the pain that shot up from his knee sickened him.

The crypt was floodlit by halogen lights that left nothing to the imagination, putting all shadows to flight.

And what they saw made Ben gasp, and Mike let out a yell of "*You bastards!*"

CHAPTER SEVEN: INSIDE THE CRYPT

The bright halogen lights illuminated more than anyone would want to see. At the far end of the crypt, Jack appeared unconscious and was spread-eagled on one of the most horrific of the instruments of torture employed by the Inquisition in its history. His hands and ankles were attached by thick leather straps, which anchored him top and bottom to the huge wooden rollers of the apparatus. The Inquisition and the Rack were alive and well.

The Prefect stood at the side of the Rack with his hands on the massive wooden crank. Beside him Monsignor Orletti was standing - his face expressionless. There were two others in the crypt, both wearing the Roman collars of the clergy, with black shirts and suits. Another stood behind them, a gun still pushed into the middle of Mike's back.

"Mr Travis, I expected you to come along. You're nothing if not predictable. As you see, your friend was unfortunate enough to be at your house when we paid you a call, Lovecraft. A shame, but then he has provided me with certain leverage. If you'll excuse the pun."

As if to emphasise his point, he gave an imperceptible tug on the crank. Jack's cry of pain lodged in both Mike and Ben, giving birth to a string of emotions from pain and rage, to an impulse to murder.

Mike swallowed and stepped closer to Jack. He felt the sting of tears behind his eyes as he looked down on Jack's beaten face; his right eye was swollen shut and below it his cheekbone stood out blue and red. His left cheek was also extensively bruised, and his eyebrow was cut. His lips were swollen, and had obviously been bleeding.

"Oh, God. Jack?"

There was a muffled murmur from Jack, which was the only response he was capable of.

Ben had remained silent, not trusting himself to try to speak. Mike shook his head and glared at the Prefect. "You know I'll make you pay for this," he said through gritted teeth.

"You can try. But in the meantime, I think my business is with Mr Lovecraft. So please, do us all a favour and shut your mouth."

Mike felt the barrel of the gun move up to the back of his neck. Undeterred, he carried on, "I'll hunt you down, wherever you think you can hide, you *son of a bitch!*"

The pressure on the back of his neck increased. The Prefect's expression didn't flicker. "Enough." He turned to Ben. "I take it this is everything?" he said, nodding towards the papers in Ben's hands.

Ben hadn't taken his eyes from the Prefect. He had recognised him the moment he had stepped into the crypt. Lucca Alessio had changed very little since Ben had last seen him in Rome, when he was just Bishop Alessio;- now he wore the black cassock piped with red. The addition of a large pectoral cross around his neck and the red skullcap proclaimed him Cardinal. His hair was silvered now but the ruthless twist to his mouth was the same, and Ben would have recognised the hard glint in his eyes anywhere. He had obviously risen rapidly and was a man well suited to his role.

Ben held out the sheaf of papers and notebooks. He spat onto the ground. "Of course this is everything. I'm not a fool."

"No. But you are a heretic, no better or worse than your friend there, who persistently pursues the occult in direct opposition to the Holy Doctrine. Bringing Satan's minions into this world is a crime against God. For which you will pay."

Ben gave a loud harsh laugh that echoed around the crypt. "And what do you call this?" he said roughly, nodding at Jack. "Is this not a crime against God?"

The Prefect shook his head. "No. It is merely a means to an end. Now, hand over the manuscript *and* your notes." His hand hovered over the crank again. Ben took in a deep breath and handed the papers to him.

The Prefect signalled to one of the others, "Search them."

They stood while they were roughly patted down and pockets searched.

"Now let him go," Ben growled, "you made a deal."

The Prefect made no response, already devouring the documents. After several minutes of heavy silence, he looked up, his dark eyes piercing Ben's.

"No," he said, "The deal, as you put it, is off. Bring me Excalibur, and bring me the evil one, the sorcerer Merlin. Bring them to me, and I will release your friend."

Mike took a step forwards, and the Prefect's hand went immediately to the crank. He barely touched it, but Jack gave a long, low moan.

"I believe that one more full turn will break his spine. Do you want me to put it to the test?" His voice was cold and even, carrying no emotion to mask his intention.

Ben countered with bravado, "That manuscript is pure medieval nonsense, useful only as literature. Do what you want with it. It's of no value."

The Prefect fixed Ben with his anthracite eyes. "You want to hope that's not the case. You really do." He gave the crank the lightest touch and Jack yelled in agony. Ben paled, and held out his hand.

"I'll need those back, in that case," he said darkly.

The Prefect raised an eyebrow. "Now it is you who takes me for a fool. You have it committed to memory, I'm sure. Or if not ..." he looked significantly at Jack.

Ben's eyes reflected the threat, "I'll go. But if anything else happens to him, Mike will have to be bloody quick to beat me to you. At least give me my notebook, I need to be sure of the words of the spell to release Merlin."

"I think not. Pray you get it right. If you remember how to pray, that is." His eyes were full of scorn, and his lip twisted into a snarl of hatred. "You have twenty four hours. I will expect you back at this time tomorrow."

"*What?* That's impossible!" Ben yelled.

"Twenty-three hours and fifty-seven seconds."

Ben looked at Jack, who appeared to have passed out. "And if I can't do it?"

"Then your friend will die."

Mike swore loudly at the Prefect and the look on his face expressed his profound rage. "I'm coming for you, you bastard."

Alessio gave a short sigh of exasperation. "You're wasting time. I believe you now have twenty-three hours and forty seconds. I should leave now, if I were you." He nodded to the man with the gun in Mike's neck.

The gun pressed into him harder, and a strong arm spun him around to face the steps out of the crypt and pushed him forwards. Ben turned with him, and together they climbed back into the daylight of the roofless ruin of Church of St. Mary the Virgin.

Behind them, the Prefect nodded at the one with the gun, Father Paolo Gambini. His silent instruction was plain. Follow them. His look added, *And don't lose them, if you know what's good for you.*

A loud crash told Mike that the trapdoor to the crypt had shut them out.

Neither of them could speak straight away, as they processed the enormity of what was before them. Eventually, Mike took out his phone and hit Beth's number on speed dial.

She answered immediately.

"Beth, listen to me. Jack is in trouble. Big trouble. And I have to go somewhere to try and fix it."

There was a moment's pause as Beth assimilated the information, "Where?" she asked.

"Glastonbury."

Her reaction was immediate and unexpected. "We're coming with you. Pick us up."

"Beth, I don't have time to come back for you, and it's not where I want Adain to be anywhere near. I'll call you again soon."

She looked around at the pile of building blocks that Adain had somehow made into a familiar shape. Glastonbury Tor, the iconic conical hill that rises from the Somerset Levels with its ruined tower on the summit, pointing heavenwards like the finger of fate. Adain began to cry and then she said, "Avalon."

"Mike! Don't you dare hang up on me! There's something you don't know, something that affects Addie. You have to *make* time. We need to come with you. Addie needs to go there too."

"Beth, just listen to me. Jack's had the shit beaten out of him, and he's being held until Ben and I do as we've been told. We've got twenty-four hours to do something that I won't even begin to try and explain right now. What's happening with Addie?"

Beth hesitated, "Then don't waste time. We'll follow you there. I'll find you." She disconnected the call before there could be any further discussion.

Mike tried to call her back but the signal had died on his phone. Beth wasn't given to flights of fancy, and if she said Addie needed something, she meant it. He'd have to wait until he saw her to find out what, although he had a pretty good idea.

Inside the crypt, Lucca Alessio slackened the tension on the rack just enough to keep Jack alive. And suffering.

CHAPTER EIGHT: FORGOTTEN SITE

Mike remained grim as he sped down the M5 motorway into Somerset, listening to Ben.

"It was Merlin who put Excalibur into the Tor, and it's only Merlin that can release it. We have to get to him first. Once we release him with his own spell from the manuscript, we can get him to retrieve it."

Mike grimaced. "Just like that! Assuming that Merlin is still alive in this crystal cave, what if he won't do it? It's not like we're even from his time. For God's sake Ben, it's been over eighteen bloody centuries since he ended up there, you think we can wake him up just like that? And why would he release Excalibur to us, when he clearly wanted it out of mortal hands?"

Ben chose his words carefully. "We have to believe he will. For Jack's sake. These people will not hesitate to take him out, Mike. They'll take all of us out, if it means their pond won't be rippled."

Mike's response was to put his foot down harder on the accelerator pedal. "You can remember the words of the spell?"

"It was in Welsh, Mike, Merlin's own language." Ben's face remained calm as he unfastened his left boot, and took out a page from his notebook. "Just to be sure," he said.

"Christ, Ben, you said you'd handed it all over. We can't mess with these assholes!"

"If they believed I wouldn't keep something back they'd be really *stupid* assholes. Without the original, which they have, my notes are worthless;- the mere ravings of an excommunicated priest. Relax Mike. My memory's good, but not that good."

"Again. This is Jack's life, we're talking about."

Ben's face clouded over. "You don't need to remind me of that."

The signpost for their exit from the motorway appeared, and they were suddenly driving through villages that appeared lost in time- Villages where you could easily imagine the cottagers and small holders eking out a living from their small patches of land, and roads bounded by ditches edged with reeds; ditches that were dug in a time long past, when man had decided to second-guess nature and drain the Somerset levels. They had dried the marshes and waters that had surrounded Avalon, before it had become Glastonbury in the outer world, and had been consigned to the mists and mystery of a different time and space. Avalon now existed only behind the veil of Glastonbury, behind the mirror of this world. And they had to break through the veil.

Mike had been in Avalon briefly. Allowed there, and taken there through the labyrinth of portals that appeared on the world grid when he'd been involved in the return of the Sacred Ark. Jack had been with him and they had left their friend Jim James there, terminally ill with a cancer that was eating away his life, leaving him in the care of the healers of Avalon. He had remained there to live out his days on the lost Isle, unable to return to this world, where the cancer would return and win the battle for his life. Only Avalon could keep it at bay.

It seemed an eternity ago, and only a distant memory, or dream, that had been placed in the far recesses of his mind. And he certainly didn't know how to get back there.

Their only hope lay in Merlin. Mike couldn't begin to contemplate the consequences of failure. And there was Adain. Whatever fate lay ahead of her, it too was connected to Avalon, or so it seemed.

Suddenly, as if out of nowhere, the tall conical hill reared up from the landscape, crowned with the ruins of St Michael's church tower. Glastonbury Tor. Even in this world it cast its spell - drawing in, connecting, mystical, and filled with magic and hope. Mike felt a tug in the centre of his chest which kindled that hope.

He turned to Ben, "Are you certain this is where Merlin is? I thought his tomb was supposed to be on Bardsey Island."

"There are several supposed resting places for him spoken of throughout the legends. Some say he lies in a forest in Brittany, some say in Scotland. But from his own prophecy in the manuscript, it's clear he was in Avalon when he encountered Nimue for the last time. He directs us to the western gateway of Avalon, to a mound that has become known as Brighid's Mound" He pronounced it *Breed's* Mound. "It's a small hill that lies on the line of earth energy, the ley that connects it with Glastonbury Tor and Stonehenge, and was once sacred to the Goddess Brigid, or Bride, depending on where you come from. The church decided to call her Saint Brigid, appropriating her from the pagans for their own. They did that a lot, in an effort to placate the Druids and the followers of the Old Religion, as they enforced their conversion. The mound is just on the western outskirts of Glastonbury itself, behind what is now an industrial estate."

The contempt in his voice for such sacrilege and neglect was obvious, but beyond that, he knew it might work in their favour. Tourists and most pagans would head for the Tor, or for the Chalice Well, where the sacred red spring surfaced, oblivious to this other sacred site - meaning they would probably be left in peace. There had been recent interest in the mound and although the land on which it lay was owned by the local council, new pilgrims had tried to reclaim the site. He hoped they were elsewhere.

Glastonbury sprawled at the foot of the Tor with new housing estates spreading its modernity ever wider. But at its core was the ruined Abbey in the centre of the town, where Arthur and Guinevere were supposed to lie. The

High Street runs from the cross in the market place leading to an entire town seemingly given over to New Age shops providing tools and accessories for the hundreds of thousands of visitors looking for answers. The old buildings chart the progress of time, from Elizabethan structures to the magnificent St. John's Church. Glastonbury drew people to it. People of all faiths and denominations, seekers of wisdom and spirituality, and those that could simply 'feel' that it was a special place. Whatever the reason for the visit to Glastonbury, people somehow came away changed somehow, however subtle.

Ben directed Mike to skirt the town and head towards Street, where the district of Beckery lay behind the crumbling red brick of an old sheepskin factory. Through an insignificant industrial estate, they followed a small lane which appeared to lead nowhere except to an old coal yard. Mike stopped the car, and raised his eyebrows and hands to shoulder height in question. Whatever preconceived image he had of an ancient sacred site near Glastonbury Tor, this wasn't it. He still had an idealised idea of a pleasant field with an obvious mound.

He tried for the second time to call Beth. No signal.

Ben nodded ahead towards a gate that appeared to lead only into a rutted and muddy field. "Over there," he said quietly.

The gate was padlocked, so they climbed over it. It seemed right somehow that their way would be barred, however slightly. The silence of the afternoon was broken only by the voices of crows in the trees bordering the field, and there seemed an unspoken acknowledgement for the need to keep it that way.

The Tor loomed up to their right - calling, reaching - and in the silence Mike felt a buzz of electricity that found a home somewhere in the middle of his chest. They were close. Confirmation came from an old stone marker leaning against the hedge, indicating that this had once been the site of Brighid's Well, now long gone.

The field was covered in nettles and brambles, and the mound was just that - a small mound - not even a hill. Mike threw a questioning glance again at Ben, who ignored him and strode on purposefully.

They approached the mound, feeling the power that ran through it, under it and from it, fed by the raw energy of the Earth Grid and the lines that connected the power places. And suddenly, this insignificant grassy mound was an appropriate resting place for Merlin of Britain.

The only sound came from a noisy rabble of crows in a hawthorn tree behind the mound. On the mound itself were the remains of obvious sacred offerings, such as Brighid's crosses, flowers, and corn dollies, all sacred to the Goddess Brighid. There was a faint air of sadness, tinged with hope of revival from the almost forgotten sacred site, but there was also a feeling of great peace. No wonder Merlin had chosen this place.

Mike tried yet again to call Beth. Again, he had no signal on his phone.

Unseen, and at a discreet distance, a car had followed them. It entered the old coal yard, and the Prefect's man, Father Paolo Gambini got out and leaned against the car, lighting a cigarette. The blue-grey smoke swirled around his white hair and face, with its mean eyes and flabby flesh. He could see Mike's car where he had left it in the lane. They were going nowhere unobserved.

CHAPTER NINE: ON BRIGHID'S MOUND

Ben took out the page of his notebook from the inside pocket of his leather biker jacket and centred himself. Whilst not a follower of the Old Religion himself, he was well used to sacred ritual and quickly put himself in the right frame of mind.

He was ready.

He lifted his arms on high, "I call upon the Gods and Goddesses of this land, on Brighid to whom this place is sacred. I come in respect, and in the name of Avalon." Then in his deep, booming voice he spoke the rich language of Merlin, intoning the words of the spell in Welsh.

"Trwy nerth y Duwiau y tir hwn, Myrddin fe'ch galwaf!
Trwy nerth y rhai hynafol, Myrddin fe'ch galwaf!
Trwy nerth gwynt y ddraig, Myrddin fe'ch galwaf!
Er mwyn Afallon, Myrddin yn dychwelyd!
Yr wyf yn eich gonsurio gan eich fedd rhwng y byd. Effro! Effro
o'r tir rhwng cysgu a deffro ac yn dychwelyd!
Yr wyf yn galw i chi yn y enw Afallon!

(By the power of the Gods of this land, Merlin I call you! By the power of the ancient ones, Merlin I call you! By the power of the dragon's breath, Merlin I call you! For the sake of Avalon, Merlin return! I conjure you from your tomb between the worlds. Awake! Awake from the land between sleeping and waking and return! I call to you in the name of Avalon!)

Mike felt a shiver down his spine and a tingle of anticipation.

Nothing happened.

Ben repeated the spell.

"Trwy nerth y Duwiau y tir hwn, Myrddin fe'ch galwaf! Trwy nerth y rhai hynafol, Myrddin fe'ch galwaf! Trwy nerth gwynt y ddraig, Myrddin fe'ch galwaf! Er mwyn Afallon, Myrddin yn dychwelyd! Yr wyf yn eich gonsurio gan eich fedd rhwng y byd. Effro! Effro o'r tir rhwng cysgu a deffro ac yn dychwelyd! Yr wyf yn galw i chi yn y enw Afallon!"

They waited.

Nothing happened.

Ben's voice grew louder and more insistent as he tried again. And again. And again.

He was sweating with the emotion that had built inside him, as the spell became a chant that took on its own rhythm, and began to resonate in both of their solar plexus.

And still nothing happened.

He lowered his arms and looked helplessly at Mike. "I don't get it. Dai and I checked and rechecked the translation, but I told you the Old Welsh is tricky and a bugger to pronounce. I didn't want to get it wrong, so this is modern Welsh, and I hoped he would understand it."

Mike sighed. "I thought you said you had it."

Ben shrugged, "I have. Maybe, he just isn't interested."

"Try again."

Ben took a deep breath and raised his arms in supplication once more. His voice was filled with the emotion of awe, and of the desperation he was now feeling. His voice rang out across the mound as he began the chant again. And again.

The change in the atmosphere was subtle at first, and neither wanted to raise their hopes. They stood in silence, hardly daring to breathe, hardly daring to hope.

Mike said quietly, "Try again."

Again Ben's voice rang out across the ether, as he, and

the spell, and the land became one.

The subtle change became stronger. Mike felt a tingling beginning in the soles of his feet, which travelled up, throughout his body. He looked at Ben, who was now totally oblivious to his surroundings. He looked down at the ground, the source of the tingling, and it appeared to shimmer, like a heat haze, despite the fact that there was no heat in the late afternoon sun.

Mike broke the silence. "Ben?"

Ben's face seemed to be losing the trance-like appearance as he focussed his eyes on Mike. "What do you think?"

"I think if that doesn't get his attention, we might as well forget it."

The heat haze began to change in structure and appearance as first it appeared to become a mist that hugged the ground, and gradually, very gradually, seemed to thicken and rise up, enveloping them, encircling the mound.

Mike was first to detect the tiny tremor from under their feet. The third tremor was unmistakable, and Ben swore softly.

The mist at the centre of the mound began to swirl and form a tall pillar as they stood before it, not a muscle moving; even the involuntary muscles of breathing were suspended. Everything around them was stilled, and the crows fell silent as if they too anticipated the manifestation of Merlin. Mike's lungs sucked in air in protest at the suspension of breath.

And they waited.

The pillar of mist began to solidify, almost taking on form, and then it suddenly dissipated, leaving nothing behind it but swirling mist around their feet. They looked at each other, as if each had an answer for what had happened. When neither was forthcoming, Mike walked over to where the pillar of mist had appeared. He looked around in frustration, then made a gesture that could have only one meaning - he was mystified.

"Think I should try again?" asked Ben.

Mike was about to concur, after all *something* had happened, it just felt incomplete. And still there was no Merlin.

Movement behind them on the hawthorn tree drew their attention. As one, the crows took flight in a noisy flurry of feathers and the reason was soon apparent. Hovering above the branches of the tree, a small falcon, head bent and wings arched downwards, glided onto the recently vacated branch. Its black eyes glinted like antique jet, and it inclined its head as if enquiring as to their presence. Mike suddenly had the feeling that they had trespassed onto holy ground, and this, the guardian of the mound, had come to see them off.

It was small for a bird of prey, but was definitely a falcon with its typical hooked beak and black beady eyes. Its brown and cream feathers ruffled in a sudden chill breeze and Mike drew his jacket closer around him, suddenly aware that if they had come to this place for nothing, then Jack was in mortal danger. They had to succeed, they had to try again. He spun around to Ben.

"Do it again. I don't care if it takes all day, do it again."

Ben shook his head; he was beginning to doubt the sanity of what they were trying to do, and worse than that - his ability to pull it off. But he rolled his thick neck and shoulders in an effort to rid himself of the negativity that had crept into him.

He cleared his throat and began to intone the spell again.

"Trwy nerth y Duwiau y tir hwn, Myrddin fe'ch galwaf! Trwy nerth y rhai hynafol, Myrddin fe'ch galwaf!"

There was a flutter of wings from the tree and the falcon gave a shrill, chattering call, then it gave a clipped note before repeating the shrill ki-ki-kee sound again. It may have been small, as birds of prey went, but its displeasure at their presence was unmistakeable.

Ben decided to ignore it and carry on.

"Trwy nerth gwynt y ddraig, Myrddin fe'ch galwaf! Er mwyn Afallon, Myrddin yn dychwelyd! Yr wyf yn eich gonsurio gan eich fedd rhwng y byd. Effro! Effro o'r tir rhwng cysgu a deffro ac yn dychwelyd! Yr wyf yn galw i chi yn y enw Afallon!"

The falcon gave its shrill alarm call again and took to the air, hovering over them momentarily before coming to land in the centre of the mound. The swirling mist seemed to engulf it, and grow dense and tall again. It was so dense, that they could no longer see the falcon, or anything else further than a foot away. From somewhere in the middle of the mist, they heard a cough and a spluttering sound, and as they strained their eyes to see into the thick vapour, it began to fade once more.

A tall man, handsome and approaching middle age, dressed in a long black woollen robe that was tied at the waist with a leather belt, stepped out of the thinning haze and as the light bulb in Ben's brain switched on, making the connections, he just managed to smother an involuntary bellow of laughter.

Merlin was renowned as a shape-shifter, frequently taking on the form of a falcon - the fact which had given rise to the bird being named after him.

The man before them looked less than happy, as he stood there pulling stray feathers from the corner of his mouth and beard, seemingly oblivious to the ones that clung to his hair. He appeared to be in his forties, and had sinfully dark eyes and a hooked nose reminiscent of the hooked beak of the bird, all set in a weathered complexion. He glared resentfully at them, and spat another offending feather onto the ground.

"Out of practice," he growled, as he coughed up another feather.

Mike leaned closer to Ben and whispered, "Well, that's not quite what I expected."

CHAPTER TEN: MORE LIKE A BROTHER

Merlin stared at them both for several minutes, appraising them with a puzzled expression. When he eventually spoke, his words came cloaked in a thick Welsh accent.

"So it's in the name of Avalon, you've called me, is it? Arthur is gone, the Goddess forgotten by her people, Britain has fallen into foreign hands, and they send *you* to call me?" His disdain was obvious. "What need does Avalon have of me?"

"Actually," said Mike, "It's not quite like that." He recounted the events that had led them there.

"Pah! Magic is not for meddling with, least of all by someone who doesn't even know when the magic is accomplished!" His words were directed at Ben, as he scowled, looking him up and down. "What mode of dress is this?" he asked tightly.

Ben grinned at him, "I'm rather afraid there is a lot that you will find strange."

"What I find strange is that you have managed to call me from the mound using my own spell!" His face cleared, "You found my parchment?"

Ben nodded. "A copy of it at least. It was hidden in Rhydderch Manor."

"Rhydderch! That name I know. I took Excalibur from his dying hand and placed it where no man could retrieve it, all except the Pendragon, - with my blessing that is. And so it appears you have called me from my rest for nothing! Excalibur is not for hands such as yours. I bid you good day!"

He started to walk away, and Mike was after him in a heartbeat. "*Where are you going?* We *need* you. Avalon may be lost in the mists between the worlds, but there is evil in the outer world, and we need your help. If you refuse, then someone I care about is going to die. How can you just walk away? Are you still in the madness that drove you into the forests?"

Merlin raised an eyebrow. "You know of that?"

"Yes. I know that the sight of so many dead in the Battle of Arfderydd, including your brothers, led you to madness."

Merlin's face darkened. "I admit, I may have been a little ... *emotional.*"

As emotional as a bag of frogs, Mike thought. He swallowed the retort, "You might have once been a power in this land, but now, in this time, you were imprisoned in that mound and we set you free. The least you can do is listen to me!" He paused and shook his head, "I can't believe I'm having this conversation. It wasn't supposed to go this way."

Merlin's penetrating gaze relaxed almost imperceptibly, and Mike thought he saw the beginnings of a smile.

"What is it you want of me?"

"I want you to take us to Avalon. I know you can do that. And I want you to give us Excalibur, and then I want you to return with us to those who are torturing my friend. A man who is more like a brother to me"

Merlin raised a dark eyebrow. "You want a great deal. Impossible. I have already told you, Excalibur is out of the reach of any but the Pendragon, and as the last Pendragon fell on the field of battle at Camlann in the north, your request is futile. I am sorry that your friend will suffer and probably die, but there is nothing that I can do. Avalon has retreated into the mists for a reason; you can't just come and go there as you please!"

"I have already been there."

Merlin stopped dead in his tracks, and turned a quizzical glance on Mike.

Mike sighed, "It's a long story."

Merlin appeared to soften, but only very slightly. "I seem to have the time."

Mike's patience came to its end. "But I don't! I have told you already - if we don't take you back with us, and with Excalibur, they will kill someone who doesn't deserve to die that way. In your time you would have called him a knight. Why does the passage of time make him less of a man?"

"So one man, even a knight, is worth the sacrifice of everything?" Merlin scowled.

There seemed little to lose, so Mike pressed on. "Arthur Pendragon would have thought so. And in any case, there will be no sacrifice. I have no intention of giving you, or the sword, to them. I read your prophecy, Merlin. You know of the rise of the New Religion, and the suffering of the people who refused to abandon the old ways. Why would you think I would let them have you? And it's true that Excalibur will defend the man who wields it."

"You speak like a warrior, but you don't look like one."

Mike sighed. "I've had my moments," he said.

Ben came up close to them and put a hand on Mike's arm. "Leave him, Mike. I'll not beg. There will be another way; we could just go back and shoot the sons of bitches."

Mike shook his hand away. "No! We've brought him back, and he can take us into Avalon. I don't know why, but I know it's what we have to do." He turned back to Merlin, "So, you have my word. I won't let the sword fall into their hands. You, I believe, can take care of yourself!"

Merlin's face creased into a smile. He was unused to being spoken to so forcefully, although he did remember one, long gone now, resting between the worlds in Avalon. "I'm going to Avalon," he said in gruff voice. "You can come if want. But I warn you, you waste your time."

He raised his hand and the mist disappeared. "By the Gods, what is this? Dry land where water should be? Is Avalon so far away?"

65

"It lies in another dimension now, parted from this world, until such a time as its healing and magic can be appreciated again and not vilified as evil. There are places close by where you can feel its presence. At the Tor and at the Chalice Well there are portals between the dimensions - gateways that I don't know how to open. I know you do."

"You know a lot."

Mike coloured. "No. I don't. But, as I told you, I have been there. I was taken there by one of the ancients." He told Merlin as briefly as he could about the Sacred Ark and his part in its return to the temple at Serabit El Khadim, to yet another parallel world.

"The Ark of the Hebrews. Yes, I know of it. Its power to maintain the integrity of the Earth Grid is also known to me. You have seen it?"

"Seen it, touched it, and sent it back. Look, I'll be happy to tell you the full story another time. But, for now, take us to Avalon. Please."

Merlin didn't reply. He simply nodded and strode along the lane. As he rounded the corner of the hedgerow, he stopped again. The Tor rose in front of them at a distance, and his eyes were fixed on the summit. The ruins of the church tower stood where once had been a stone circle with a tall standing stone at its centre.

"Glastonbury," said Mike. "Avalon lies somewhere behind it, mirrored in its energy."

Merlin's face tightened again. He'd been happier in his enforced imprisonment, apart from the unwelcome changes in the outer world. He regretted having committed his spell to parchment, and he regretted even more that it had been put to use. Above all else he craved the sanctuary of the Isle of Priestesses.

"I know the portals, and how to open them. And I am one who can call the barge that will take us to Avalon. Tell me about your friend. He is a knight, you say?"

Ben grinned at him again, and allowed himself a not-so-subtle laugh. "You've been asleep a long time Merlin," he said. "A great deal has changed."

"I have seen many changes in visions whilst I slept within the crystal. Dreams you may call them, but I have seen the wars and ravages that have torn this land apart. Many of them I foretold in my prophecies. I have seen horses replaced by belching iron beasts that poison the air, and lesser kings and queens upon the throne of England." He lowered his voice, "My time was done long ago; I have no place here. You should not have awoken me. I must go to Avalon. I know not if you will be welcome there, but you may come with me if you wish."

Merlin paused and looked over his shoulder towards the coal yard. So, these two had enemies that were already nearby. He narrowed his eyes, and decided to say nothing. But he would watch.

He returned to the centre of the mound and stood, arms raised, head lowered, in silence. He remained that way for several minutes. Everywhere was hushed. Mike and Ben moved in closer, suddenly aware of another shift in the atmosphere. The air seemed tighter somehow, and then, as suddenly as it had dissipated, the mist returned.

Merlin was mumbling incoherent words in a language that they had never heard before - the language of magic. Then he suddenly lifted his head, face to the heavens, and his voice rang out in tones that sent waves of energy moving outwards in concentric circles. Through the fingers of mist, the circles made their way to Avalon. This time, Ben knew the language. Merlin was speaking in his native tongue, Welsh, the lilting, rich language of the Cymru.

"Ffordd o amser, nid wyf bellach eich clywed. Ffordd o le i mi wneud cais i chi agor y Baedd! Ffordd o gyfarfod o amser a gofod, Gwrandewch arnaf fi ac yn gwneud fy orchymyn! Agor y ffordd i Afallon. Yr wyf yn Myrddin Prydain gorchymyn ei."

Ben automatically translated the words in his head.

Way of time, I no longer hear you! Way of space, I bid you open the Boar! Way of meeting of a time and space, hear me and do my command! Open the way to Avalon! I, Merlin of Britain command it!

Disorientation was instant, accompanied by an intense dragging sensation in their solar plexus. It was over in a heartbeat.

The figure standing in the coal yard made the sign of the cross over his chest and dived inside the car. The mist had descended again, thicker and denser, and he could no longer see his quarry. But as he turned the key in the ignition, the fog cleared again, falling to the ground and disappearing into the field. Of Mike and Ben there was no sign, but their car was still parked where they had left it.

He'd lost them.

His only chance now lay in Glastonbury. At the Tor. He turned his car out of the coal yard and headed for the mystical hill.

The mist still swirled around Mike and Ben's feet. Merlin raised his arms above his head until his palms met, fingers outstretched. Then, with a sudden movement, he turned his hands so that his palms faced the ground, and very slowly lowered them to his side, all the time muttering unintelligible words. As he lowered his hands, it seemed as though they took the mist with them.

Mike and Ben looked out from the mound, which was now a small island in the middle of mist-covered water that stretched before them, and all around them. The outskirts of Glastonbury had gone, and in the distance, ahead of them, the conical hill with its labyrinth of terraces, rose from the mists, topped with a stone circle, in the centre of which a tall standing stone reached towards the sky. Avalon.

CHAPTER ELEVEN: WAY PAST COMPLICATED

Adain had picked up on Beth's anxiety and was fretful as her mother hurried around, throwing things into a large holdall. Like any mother, Beth knew that taking a small child anywhere required the level of preparation for going on safari, or a canoe trip up the Amazon.

It had been two hours since Adain's block had knocked her senseless, and she had seen and heard Morgan La Fey, or Morgana, the Lady of Avalon. And even longer since she had spoken to Mike. Now she wondered what she was doing; knee-jerk reactions were uncharacteristic, as was panic. They had watched Adain carefully since the day they made the tenuous connection between her accelerated development and Grace, whose gifts had been muted until the time she had needed to use them to power the Sacred Ark, during Mike's involvement in Sinai. Somewhere, deep inside, they had always known that Adain was different. Just how different was only now apparent. With a sigh, Beth put the kettle on the hob; a cup of tea would always lift her spirits.

It had been the feeling in her heart when she had spoken with Morgana that had shown her the truth - Adain needed help from Avalon. Beth's beloved Goddess and God of the pagans had been put aside temporarily in favour of the Christian faith, to the point of Beth becoming an ordained priest. It had been her response to being beaten, and continuously told that her Old Religion was evil. Now she understood that whatever, and however, one approached the divine, along whichever path, the destination was the same. And with that understanding had come peace; peace enough to return to her first love of the deities of the Old Religion. So having a 'conversation' with the one who spoke for her Goddess on the Isle of Avalon had been the reason for her flurry of activity. Now she pulled it back a notch, had it simply been the product of her imagination in lost consciousness? She dialled Mike's number. It went to voicemail. She frowned, *Damn him*.

Adain pulled her from her reverie, in the corner of Beth's eye she saw the steaming kettle levitate and wobble as Addie said 'Tea, please Mummy.' Her instincts told her not to react and distract her daughter's attention, which could mean a shower of boiling water as she lost control of the kettle. She moved slowly towards her and pulled her clear a millisecond before the predicted shower of scalding water, hugging her close and rocking her in the slow, gentle rhythm that comes naturally to a mother. "Oh, Addie, what can we do to help you?" she whispered into her daughter's hair.

Instinctively, she knew the truth of Morgana's words: that help lay in Avalon. Morgana had said that a priestess of the Isle was on her way to escort them there and Beth hoped she would come soon as Mike would be looking for them in Glastonbury. Things were way past complicated, and if it had been anyone other than Jack who had pulled Mike away at this time, she would have resented it. Mike hadn't said exactly what kind of trouble that Jack was in, but she knew it must be serious. Holding her child close, she prayed to the Goddess for both of them.

She was relieved to hear the door-bell ring. A tall and willowy woman with long red hair beamed at her. As she moved, the light caught the inner fire of the crystal at her throat, a crystal the colour of a kingfisher's wing, with an inner light that resembled a tiny star caught at its heart.

"Hello, I'm Rowan," she said. Her voice had a musical quality, reminding Beth of the sound of a harp. Beth warmed to her immediately.

"Oh, I'm so glad you've come. Please, come in." Her brow furrowed, "How *did* you get here?"

Rowan laughed, and again Beth was reminded of the ripple of harp strings. "We have many friends in your world. One such friend brought me here, but he couldn't stay, I'm afraid."

The living room was filled with autumn sunshine streaming through the large window. "You have a lovely home, Beth." She turned to Adain. "And you must be Adain. Why, you're just beautiful." She knelt down onto the floor beside her. "Would you like to come with Mummy and see where *I* live?"

Adain treated Rowan to her best smile, and nodded energetically. "Yes, please! Can Bear come with us?" As if to emphasise her wish, she pointed at the teddy bear that had become her constant companion. It flew towards her and caught her in the eye, bringing forth a cry of anguish followed by floods of tears. Beth picked her up with distress in her eyes.

Rowan became instantly serious. "Of course Bear can come. I was hoping he would want to. Shall we help Mummy to get ready?"

Adain sniffled and nodded, clutching her teddy under her arm. "Can Daddy and Jack come too?"

Beth nodded significantly towards the kitchen door. "Can we have a quick talk?" She whispered in Adain's ear, "Addie, will you go and get your shoes on?" Still sniffing, Adain wriggled free of Beth's arms and toddled towards the hallway.

"Rowan, Mike is in Glastonbury. I have no idea what has happened to our friend Jack, but Mike said he was in bad trouble. Then he goes racing off to Glastonbury. I said I would meet him there."

"Then we had better not waste any more time. Are you ready?"

Beth nodded, her misery written on her face in capital letters.

The journey to Glastonbury was a more sedate affair than Mike's. For one thing, Beth's old Morris Minor

Traveller - whilst pretty and nostalgic to look at, and adequate for her daily needs - displayed its age and displeasure when Beth's right foot pressed down too hard. The other thing was that Beth relaxed as soon as her concentration was on the road, and not on the chaos that was threatening to engulf her. Rowan chatted to her brightly, describing Avalon and how it was reached from Glastonbury.

"Your scientists are beginning to agree that there are several dimensions to the same reality. Worlds folded upon each other. They also know that there are places where the different worlds are so close, they almost touch. It's these places that can give us access to another dimension. They appear at the sacred places on your earth, where the ancient ones knew the power of these sites. Avalon and Glastonbury lie very close, or at least they did, before this world pushed it away into the mists. But we live in the hope that one day ..." she looked at Adain in the rear view mirror, asleep and cuddling her teddy, "The energy of Glastonbury Tor is magnified in Avalon, where the sacred power has remained unpolluted. In your world, people are again beginning to feel that power there, and many in this world are hearing the voice of the Goddess again. Long ago, the worlds overlapped there, until she and the old Gods were banished from your land. I know you are one of those who carry her in your heart, Beth. Put your faith in her. Morgana will take Adain to the stone circle at the top of the Tor, and will use that energy to still what is happening to her until she has the understanding to be able to control it. It's a gift, Beth. One that she will be able to use to heal the wounds of those days. She will be fine." She chose her next words carefully. "It will always be a matter of free choice, Beth. No-one is going to take her from you. Morgana told me that your husband also has a special gift and that his journey would take him to Avalon too. I'm sure that whatever has happened to your friend is connected with that."

Beth turned to her. "I hope you're right." She needed to change the subject. "How long have you been in Avalon? Tell me about it."

Another ripple of harp strings made Beth smile. "I was born there. My mother was a priestess and I was schooled in the old ways. She taught me everything she knew about the herbs and how they are used in magic and healing. I serve the Goddess there as one of the healers."

"Then why aren't you the one to be the next Lady of Avalon? Why do you all seem to believe it's to be Addie?" Her voice trembled with emotion tinged with a heady blend of anger, fear and resentment.

"Because it has long been prophesised that it will be one with a foot in both worlds, the daughter of a warrior and a follower of the old ways. If Avalon is to be prevented from disappearing forever into the mists, and connection with your world severed forever, it is going to take one who is born of this world with the gifts that she has. Beth, you will be able to make the decision together when she is older - Avalon is not so cruel as to deny you that right. Until then, we can help her by damping down these gifts in the way I have told you."

"Will I be able to go to the stone circle with her?"

"Well, of course. I expect that Morgana will also take some of our little ones too so that Adain will not be frightened by the energy there, although I doubt that will be the case. She's beautiful Beth, and whatever happens, she will become a beautiful woman."

Beth seemed slightly mollified as she shifted in her seat, leaning back and trying to relax again. "Tell me about Avalon," she said.

"Avalon lies in the Severn Sea, or the Summer Sea, as some call it. Your Severn Estuary is much diminished from when it was known as a sea. The land around the isle is marshland, and small islands in the middle of mist enshrouded water and wetlands. It was first inhabited by the ancients that had fled and survived the destruction of a place you call Atlantis. They stayed secluded there, nurturing the land and their magic. The Old Religion flourished there and remains there still. Once only priestesses lived there, and then Druids arrived and were made welcome. Then came the priests of the New Religion, and in the spirit that is Avalon, they too were made welcome, until the day arrived when they weren't satisfied to live alongside us in peace, but they tried to enforce their beliefs and practices on us. It was then that Avalon faded into the mists, to protect it and the old ways, and to perpetuate the worship of the Goddess and the old Gods."

Beth was visibly relaxing, listening to the hypnotic quality of Rowan's obvious love for Avalon and all it stood for.

Rowan continued. "At the foot of the Tor are fields and orchards that always blossom and fruit with no help from human hands. Beyond them is a settlement of huts and houses which are our homes. There is a central Meeting House, a house where the young priestesses live and are taught, and a house where the Druids live. Not many of us leave Avalon for the outer world, but some do. Those that leave usually return to the peace that is Avalon."

It wasn't long before the M5 motorway had eaten up the miles and suddenly, to the left on the horizon, the tall conical hill rose in the distance. Beth felt the tug of it in the middle of her chest, along with the strange fascination that it held for all who gazed on it.

CHAPTER TWELVE: AN OLD FRIEND

At the edge of Brighid's Mound, Merlin lifted his head, and once again he spoke in his native Welsh.

"Galwaf ar y cwch o Afallon. I, Myrddin Prydain yn ceisio mynediad i Ynys Afallon Sanctaidd."

I call the barge of Avalon. I, Merlin of Britain seek entrance to the Sacred Isle of Avalon.

He seemed to relax momentarily, appearing satisfied with his work, although his expression still brought to mind an approaching thunder storm.

Mike ignored the dark flash from Merlin's eyes. "So, what now?"

"Now we wait," was the terse reply.

Only minutes later they heard a soft, rhythmic, lapping sound behind the reeds that grew close to the shore, veiled in the mist that obscured their vision. Seconds later, the prow of a low barge pierced the mists. The lapping sound ceased as the barge of Avalon slid silently towards the bank.

Two young priestesses were at the oars and a young woman with Celtic beauty stood in the prow. She gathered up the hem of her long, green woollen dress, and stepped lithely from the barge onto the bank. She approached Merlin with obvious reverence and lowered her head.

"Merlin of Britain, I am Estreya and I bring you the blessings of Avalon. You are welcome." She turned to Mike and Ben and bowed briefly, "You too, are welcome in Avalon. Morgana has sent me to guide you through the mist. The way can be treacherous for those who don't know the bogs and the marshes."

The barge slid forwards into the mist, a rhythmic lapping accompanying the strokes of the oars. Water fowl took to the air as the barge approached, drawing silently towards the shore of Avalon.

At the shore the mists gave way to lush grass, leading into vast orchards laden with their autumn fruit. Avalon, the Isle of Apples. One of the young priestesses jumped onto the wooden landing stage and tied up the barge for them to alight. Merlin's scowl seemed to lift as he stepped onto the sacred ground.

As they made their way through the orchards into autumn sunshine, Mike saw a man coming towards them. A man he knew well. A friend who should be dead, but now appeared in excellent health.

Jim James used to be a copper. A dying copper. And when Mike was in the kind of trouble that could have put him away until his beard was white, Jim had done the right thing instead of the legal thing, and stood by Mike and his family. Then he had gone with Mike and Jack into Sinai in search of the Sacred Ark - it was to be his last hurrah, his terminal cancer bringing his end within touching distance.

None of them could have predicted that at the end of that expedition they would be returning from the ancient temple in Sinai via a portal to Avalon, where Jim would remain under the care of the healers of that Isle.

He strode towards them, hair still iron grey and his grey bristly moustache still his trademark. His face remained weathered but now had a healthy tan, and the sallow skin and yellowing eyes were replaced by sparkling eyes and a broad smile. Mike was genuinely shocked. Ten years seemed to have been removed from his friend.

He pulled Jim to him, and put his arms around his friend's shoulders with a look of such genuine pleasure that no-one spoke to interrupt the reunion.

"Jim! You're a sight for sore eyes! How the hell are you?"

Jim's broad grin grew wider. "See for yourself, Mike! I'm well. I'm really well; I guess you'd say I'm healed." He saw the puzzled look on Mike's face and broke into a hoarse laugh. "What? You thought I'd be dead by now? Hell if I know! They tell me I can never leave this place, but look around you!" He made an expansive gesture. "I've got everything I need here. Beautiful women have healed my body and my mind. And that's the key Mike, healing the mind. And this place has healed my soul. So why would I ever *want* to leave here?" He smiled at Ben and Merlin, and looked at Mike in expectation of an introduction.

Mike was suddenly aware that he had totally ignored Ben during this happy reunion. He made amends.

"Jim, this is another friend of mine and Jack's, Ben Lovecraft." Jim and Ben exchanged pleasantries. "And this is ... um ... Merlin."

Jim seemed unfazed by the introduction; he put out a hand to Merlin. "Of course it is. I'm honoured to meet you, Sir." He turned back to Mike. "Come with me, Mike. The Lady is waiting for you."

"The Lady?" Mike queried.

Jim smiled again, and again Mike was shaken at his healthy appearance. "Morgana, Mike. Or you may know of her as Morgan Le Fey. You'll need to speak up a bit though. She's extremely old and a little deaf, though she doesn't accept that," he laughed. "But her mind is as still as keen as any fairy-forged blade."

Mike raised an eyebrow.

Jim laughed again, "You think I could live here without learning a thing or two? Thinking outside the box won't cut it. Think outside the planet and maybe you'll come close." He clapped Mike on the back, "Come on. It's not polite to keep a lady waiting; Estreya is to take you straight to her."

By unspoken understanding, Ben remained with Jim and was taken to the Meeting House, where a large circular table was laid with food and wine from Avalon's vines. Merlin had suddenly disappeared and Mike guessed, quite correctly, that he was already with Morgana - and probably putting his point of view forward that no way should Mike be allowed to get his hands on Excalibur.

As Estreya and Mike approached Morgana's house, which stood apart from the rest of the settlement, they could hear his raised voice, which owed nothing to consideration of Morgana's failing hearing. Merlin was nothing if not forceful in his opinion.

"We have no idea *what* will happen if Excalibur is free in the outer world again! We have no way of trusting this man. I agree with you that the Inquisition has many sins to answer for, but it's not our job to ..." His voice trailed off as Mike entered the long, low wooden house of The Lady of Avalon.

Mike had not had the privilege of meeting her the last time he was in Avalon, but his visit then had been brief and deemed to be 'passing through'. He had long since given up on preconceived ideas, but after Jim's warning that Morgana was extremely old, he was unprepared for her startling beauty. Her hair was pure white, pulled loosely into her neck and fastened with a leather barrette. She wore a long, aqua woollen dress, and around her neck she wore a beautifully tooled silver locket in the centre of which was a moonstone of astonishing gem quality. It was her only adornment, but she needed none. Her eyes were kind but penetrating, and Mike shifted from foot to foot as he felt her glance read every inch of his being. He smiled back at her, and instantly felt like a foolish schoolboy in front of the headmistress. Morgana sat on a wooden chair in front of her fireplace and indicated that Mike should take the one facing her. Merlin stood at her shoulder, glaring into the flames in the hearth. He was not a happy Merlin.

Right then Mike didn't care who he may, or may not, offend, and his situation, that would probably have sent others screaming for medication, left him unmoved. It wasn't his first rodeo, as they say. But he was humbled by the gently spoken old woman, who waited patiently for his request.

Without thought, Mike lowered his head briefly out of respect for her. "I expect that Merlin has told you why I have come here. I apologise that it is an uninvited intrusion, but I have need - a friend has great need - of Avalon's help. There are people in our world who seek to eradicate all but their own doctrines, deeming all others false or downright evil. They stop at nothing to accomplish, by any means, the removal of anything, and anybody, that they consider heresy. And they pretty much consider everything that way. I know that I am asking a great deal of you, and of Merlin, and I have absolutely no idea of how I will be able to keep Excalibur from them. All I know is that I have to take it to them so that they will release my friend. I give you my word that I will not let Excalibur fall into their hands permanently."

Merlin snorted. Morgana gave him a look that brought his silence. Still she said nothing. Still she continued to lock her penetrating eyes into Mike. Still she smiled with compassion and gentleness at him.

Eventually, she said, "Is that it? Are you finished?"

Mike nodded miserably. He could see his failure on the horizon, and he daren't go anywhere near thinking about what might happen to Jack because if it. He was in no doubt whatsoever that if he failed, Jack was going to die.

She continued, "Avalon will do all that it can to help you." Merlin made a noise that brought Morgana's hand up to silence him again. Mike beamed at her, but again her hand was raised, to silence him and not Merlin this time. "Avalon will do whatever it can to help you, because your fate and the fate of your child are linked with ours. But it is not for us alone to grant you Excalibur. When Merlin took it from Rhydderch at the end of the battle, he cast it into the heart of the Tor, where it remains, guarded by the one whose decision it will be. And then there is Nimue." She glanced at Merlin. "She too has awoken. And I'm afraid she also wants the return of Excalibur. Her words and deeds have been hard indeed since she broke with Avalon, since the day she battled with you, my old friend, Merlin of Britain. She seeks to be my successor, but it is not for her to take on my mantle." She turned her gaze to Mike. "That destiny is the destiny that forges links between us. Adain, your daughter, carries the genetic code of Avalon from her mother and it is she that is destined to succeed me. For that, and other considerations, you have our support."

Before Mike could protest, Merlin stepped in front of Morgana. "Nimue? She is here?" he demanded.

There was a fire in his eyes that was born of love, and lust, and passion, as he remembered his love for her. And how she had betrayed that love. Mike couldn't restrain the thought of how often it was that the good guy fell for the bad girl. The thought was gone as quickly as it formed, as he watched Merlin begin to pace in front of Morgana. He suddenly felt irrelevant. The stage was Merlin's now.

"Nimue was and always will be The Lady of the Lake. If she is here then I must see her."

Morgana's eyes saddened as she watched Merlin's torture. Her heart hardened against Nimue even further. "She isn't here, Merlin. She broke with Avalon long ago, before that fateful day. Your spell of protection was so powerful that her own spell rebounded on her, and she has slept too. Not in Avalon, nor in the outer world, but between the worlds."

"Where is she now, Morgana?"

The Lady of Avalon shook her head. "I don't know. I'm sorry, Merlin."

The conversation was halted as there was a flurry of activity outside. Estreya left quickly, and returned with as much haste.

"Lady, please come."

Her face was grave as she went to Morgana's side.

"What is it, child?" Morgana's concern was obvious; Estreya always carried herself with quiet dignity. It would take something of magnitude to cause such agitation.

"It's Rowan, Lady. She has been found near the red spring. She is unconscious, and it appears that she is the victim of dark and powerful magic. We cannot wake her. She is safe in the infirmary now." She paused momentarily, and then she said, almost in a whisper, "Her crystal is gone."

The word on Morgana's lips was already echoing through Merlin's head.

Nimue.

CHAPTER THIRTEEN: A COMPLEX SOUL

Shape-shifting was one of the first of Merlin's arts that he had shared with Nimue. And she was good at it.

So good, that she could take on the appearance, and voice, of any living creature. Rowan had been easy.

The gentle healer had been preoccupied as she approached the sacred red spring of healing waters to obtain a blessing before departing into the outer world, and she was caught unawares when the Lady of the Lake appeared before her. Her surprise had been cut short as Nimue's magick hit her full on, and she fell to the floor in a crumpled heap. Nimue bent over her, and wrenched the crystal from her neck.

When she stood, she had taken on the exact appearance of Rowan.

The red-stained rocks around the spring had only served to compound Nimue's evil, as Rowan's head had connected with the jagged granite. A trickle of blood ran from her temple, down the side of her face, and pooled in her neck. Rowan was going nowhere. But she, Nimue, was going to collect the Successor.

Now she was close to her goal. If Morgana insisted on taking this infant as her successor, then she would do so knowing that it had been she, Nimue, who had reared her. In her own ways, and doing her will.

Adain had been asleep for most of the journey but she awoke suddenly. The Tor was closer now, and its energy was reaching out to Beth, drawing her in, ever closer. She sensed Adain's sudden wakefulness, and looked at her in the rear view mirror, knowing that she too could feel the pull of the conical hill.

"Hi Addie," she crooned. "Sleepy-head. We're almost there, and we'll go and find Daddy."

Adain was looking straight ahead, and pointing towards the ever-nearing Tor. "Avalon," she said.

Beth had just driven through the village of Street which had almost become part of Glastonbury over time, and Nimue asked her to pull over. They were approaching the southern portal of Avalon where she would bring down the mists and call the barge. To take them not to Avalon, but to the Isle of Godney to the north. Godney was one of the seven sacred isles, whose relative positions replicated the stars of the Great Bear. It was uninhabited, and would serve as a suitable refuge whilst she negotiated her demands.

They left Beth's car in a small pull-in on the lane. Beth took Adain from the car and pulled on her warm coat. It had been sunny all the way, but now as the sun began its descent into the west, there was a chill in the air.

Nimue stood on top of a small mound and began her chant. The soothing ripple of harp music filled Beth, and as the mists descended, she and Adain fell under her spell. Nimue would not risk a tantrum from the child that would bring about the force of her power, nor the interference of her mother. They were under her control, and once on the Isle of Godney they would fall asleep.

In Avalon, Estreya draped Morgana's cloak around her and they left immediately with Merlin. Mike felt helpless as he waited for an escort to take him back to Ben and Jim.

He had expected another priestess to come for him, and was surprised when a young boy of about twelve appeared in the doorway. His name was Bron, he said, and he informed Mike with pride that he was undergoing schooling with the Druids. He chatted amiably to Mike as they made their way past the clutch of similar dwellings to the Meeting House where Ben was still sitting at the laden table, engrossed in passionate conversation with Jim.

They both stood as Mike approached, eager for news

of the outcome of the meeting. Mike told them of Rowan's discovery, something that had obviously created alarm for reasons they had chosen not to tell him.

He sat down heavily on the bench next to Ben, as Jim poured a glass of wine and handed it to him, concern lining his face. Mike took it gratefully and suddenly realised that he was hungry.

But more than that, he was exhausted.

Jim was deeply affected by the news of Rowan's attack. She was the senior healer, not by dint of age, but because of her amazing skill, and the knowledge that had turned into experience over time. Her mother had carried that honour before her, and from the time Rowan could walk and understand her mother, she had begun her training. Throughout his time in Avalon, Jim had seen more of Rowan than any other.

"Mike, I'm sorry about Jack. Ben just finished telling me about it: about why you are here. I should've known it wasn't because you missed me!" His efforts to make light of their situation failed dismally. "Look, do you mind very much if I go to the infirmary to see if there's anything I can do?"

Mike knew the implications of that look - Jim was in love with Rowan. He grinned at Jim, as they both agreed without hesitation, and Jim left them immediately.

"No need to ask how it went," said Ben. Mike's face said everything.

Mike shrugged, "Well, Morgana said that they would do what they could to help. But Merlin still isn't convinced. And apparently the decision has to be made by someone else. God knows who! But they've gone to the infirmary for now."

"Guess we just wait, then. You should get something to eat. Trust me, it's good." Ben smiled encouragement at Mike and was rewarded by seeing his friend fill a pewter plate with chicken, cheese and fruit.

After Mike had rekindled some strength and visibly

relaxed, Ben poured him another terracotta goblet of wine.

Ben leaned forwards on his elbows, "Don't be too hard on Merlin, Mike. He's a complex soul. There's more to him than merely having been King Arthur's wizard."

Mike frowned. "Convince me."

"We first hear of Merlin from Geoffrey of Monmouth, in his '*History of the Kings of Britain*' and his other work '*The Life of Merlin*', about his dealings with King Vortigern. Vortigern wanted to build a fortress in Snowdonia, but every time they began the walls would collapse. He sent for the Druids in the end, to see if they had an answer. They told Vortigern that he should pour the blood of a child with no father onto the stone walls. So he sent out his army to find such a child. They found Merlin in Carmarthen; the town that was latterly named after Merlin. Caer Myrddin - now Carmarthen - means Merlin's Tower. His name was Emrys, and he was a child that the other kids called Fatherless. He was in fact the son of a princess, but his father was one of the Faerie race."

Mike was getting restless. "Is there any point to this story?"

Ben ignored him and carried on. "As Vortigern was about to spill his blood, Merlin told him the problem was, that under the place he wanted to build, two dragons lived and fought. One red, one white. It was their furious battles that were causing the walls to fall down. Vortigern ordered the place to be excavated, and the dragons flew out and continued their fighting in the sky overhead. It was then that Emrys made his first prophecy, and Vortigern was so impressed he spared Emrys, who was later to become known as Merlin. Emrys told Vortigern that the red dragon represented the Welsh, the white one the English, and they would continue fighting until one of them was victorious - which he said would be the Welsh. Its history now that this is what happened. It was when he was grown that he became involved in the Battle of Arfderydd, after which as you know, he became Merlin the Wild, living in the woods among nature and making his prophesies. Later, he became the Merlin everyone knows about - the wise counsellor to Arthur. It was Merlin who designed and organised the construction of the round table."

"What about Nimue?" Mike asked. "There seems to be a bit of history, to say the least."

"Ah, the beautiful and treacherous Lady of the Lake. Well that story is as old as time. Merlin fell for her in the biggest way possible. She enchanted him, and drove his passions, as they say." He laughed. "She seduced him into giving her all of his magic, and then wanted the glory and the power for herself, so she tried to kill him. The result is the other part of his story that's well known. Her magic backfired and instead of death, he found himself imprisoned in the crystal cave. Until the other day." He paused, "Mike, at one time the whole of Britain was known as Merlin's Land, such was the respect he inspired."

Mike was quiet as he pondered the wisdom of Merlin's guidance. He drained his goblet of wine. "Good enough," he said.

Ben shifted in his seat and his expression became serious. "Mike, about Jack and I ..."

Mike sat back and scrutinized Ben's face. "Do I need to hear this?" he asked with a grin.

"Yes. Yes, I think you do. I know how much Jack means to you, and I need you to know that he means no less to me. I know you both go way back, and Jack says that you're more of a brother than a friend. There are things you need to know about me, I need you to trust me."

Mike tilted his head. "I think trust has been established already, don't you? There aren't many people that would trust me to kill them and then bring them back." He was referring to the exorcism of Victoria Little, when he and Ben had battled the demon Ahriman together. "Look, Ben, all I need to know is that you care about Jack. Spare me the details, eh?" He gave Ben a weak smile. Jack was the whole reason for them being there. Both were prepared to go where it took them to get him free. Mike had always known that Jack was gay, but the fact meant as much to him as the fact that he had green eyes. Jack was Jack and that was it.

His initial concern, that Jack and Ben were a distinctly odd couple, had been dissipated as he had come to know Ben better. Jack was tall, slim and tanned, with sandy hair and an infectious smile that framed perfect white teeth. He had lived the life of the stereotypical playboy since leaving the RAF, the victim of government cut backs and redundancies. He had taken his financial handshake, and added it to family money to create his successful helicopter charter business out of Cardiff Airport. He loved fast cars, and his exclusive apartment overlooking Cardiff Bay. In contrast, Ben was a huge bear of a man, who dressed in keeping with the local chapter of Hell's Angels, in black leather trousers and boots, white shirts and black leather waistcoat and jacket. His red beard was grizzled and long and matched his hair, which was usually contained in a bandana. He was a qualified psychiatrist and an excommunicated Catholic priest. Rebel was in his DNA. He lived with his Rottweiler, Fred, in an isolated cottage with no electricity or running water. Chalk and cheese.

All that mattered was that they both cared about Jack. Mike didn't need to know the details, but it looked as if Ben was in the mood for confidences.

"I don't know, Mike, I think it's this place. It kind of brings out the need for truth and openness, don't you think?" He didn't wait for a reply, there was no need. "You know that I was an ordained priest, and that I left the Church because we didn't see eye to eye on things. Especially on their constant need for control over the masses, and the way that control is played out. But when I was ordained, Mike, I made those promises to God, not to the Church. And they still stand. Do you understand what I'm saying?"

Mike was terribly afraid that he did, and that Ben was about to explain why he and Jack were too far apart in crucial areas for their relationship to work. He didn't know if he was angry or sad. Ben read his expression, and grinned at him.

"I took a vow of celibacy, Mike. Not as a compliance with a church ruling, but it was my personal sacrifice to God. I made that promise and yes, at times it's been difficult, but nothing like the situation I find myself in now. I've spent hours, days, weeks, months, trying to come to terms with this, and I always come back to the same thing. I made the promise to God. Not the God of the Churches, or any organised religion, but God *inside*. Do you understand?"

Mike did. He could only nod his understanding, now unsure of where this was going.

"The thing is, Jack and I have talked for just as many hours, and the fact is that he's okay with it. When we get him back, and we *will* get him back, he's going to move into the cottage. I love him, Mike. I just wanted you to know, that's all."

Mike sighed his relief, and grinned at Ben. "I thought for a minute you were going to tell me that I'd have a reason to hurt you. Bad." He laughed, and took a gulp of wine.

"Never." Ben looked up as Merlin and Morgana entered the Meeting House. "Here comes news. And it doesn't look good."

CHAPTER FOURTEEN: MORE THAN A RESCUE MISSION

Morgana's face was grave as she approached with Merlin on one side and Estreya, the other. None of them looked as though they were about to share a good joke.

Mike and Ben stood as they neared the circular table.

Morgana sat, but Mike and Ben remained standing. "Rowan is awake, thanks to her assistants, although I'm afraid she has confirmed my earliest fears. Nimue was here, very briefly, or I would have known it. She was here just long enough to take Rowan's crystal and her shape, and to remove her from her duty. It is that duty that I must talk to you about."

Her face was grave and she was obviously choosing her words carefully.

"Rowan was on her way to your home in the outer world, to escort your wife and your daughter here. Please," she said as Mike's protest birthed in his throat. "Please, hear me out. You will know by now that Adain has very special gifts. Gifts, that if left unchecked, will do her harm, and those around her. They need to be calmed until such time as she is properly prepared to handle them. She has the power of telekinesis, Michael; I have seen the result of her moving things with her mind with no control over the object. But you may not know that she also has the power of telepathy. I can see you wondering how I can have seen this. It is simply that I can see through the veil, and observe what is happening in your world. The red spring flows into a pool of such beauty and calm, it is easy to use it to 'see'.

Mike was about to interrupt her again, but her glance made him resist the urge.

91

Morgana said, "I saw Adain move one of her wooden bricks with her mind, then lose control over it, and it hit Beth on the temple rendering her unconscious." Again she stilled Mike's alarm by her raised hand. "She is fine, a nasty lump, but she's fine. While she was in the receptive state of unconsciousness, I went to her in a vision and explained to her that Adain needed to come here. I also knew that she was coming to Glastonbury to meet you and I prevailed upon her to wait for an escort. Rowan was that escort." She waited for it all to sink in.

"Where are they?" he demanded.

"At this moment in time, I do not know their whereabouts ..."

Mike was past good manners. "So go to your damn pool and look! If you can do what you say, go and look!"

Ben put a steadying hand on his arm, which was promptly shaken off. Morgana looked weary, and every day of her countless years. Estreya moved silently close to her, and glared at Mike. "Please do not speak so to the Lady of Avalon. It is not her fault that Nimue has chosen the path of dark magic against the honour of Avalon. Your daughter is as dear to us as any of our priestesses, and more so."

Mike was on a roll now, and no amount of diplomacy was going to stem the tide.

"My daughter has nothing to do with this place! And never will have! I am here only to save my friend, my ... brother ... from death in the vilest way imaginable. As far as I'm concerned, Avalon can go to hell and back! My daughter is off limits. Do you understand? Now, either you go and look into your damn pool and tell me where they are or ...," his words failed him at the enormity of what had happened in his absence. Once again, Beth and Adain were in danger because of his actions. His guilt would take no prisoners.

Morgana seemed to lose some of her regal bearing and appeared to take on the hunched posture of an old woman. Estreya fussed over her.

When Merlin spoke, they were shocked at the change in him. Gone was the grumpy bad temper, and gone was the resentment at his awakening. He was Merlin of Britain again.

"Firstly, you will apologise for your undeserved rudeness to Morgana. Secondly, if you want to find your wife and daughter *and* claim Excalibur, you will put away your anger and come with me, instead of covering yourself in guilt and self-pity. There is much to do."

Merlin had read him perfectly, and Mike had been instantly sorry for his outbreak of temper towards an old woman, he knew there was no excuse for it, and he knew that Merlin was right. Directing his anger outwards assuaged his guilt for only a nanosecond.

He moved close to Morgana, and Estreya was instantly in front of her, protecting her. Mike smiled at her obvious devotion. She moved aside with caution, and a glance that would have put fear into a pissed-off gorilla with a flick-knife.

He lowered his eyes momentarily, choosing his words carefully, unwilling to be seen as offering an act of false contrition. "I humbly apologise, Lady."

Morgana smiled and patted his hand. "It is understandable. We will find them and bring them here to safety, of that I promise you. With regard to your other dilemma, I believe that Merlin has a solution. You *must*, however, listen to him, and the path is not for the faint-hearted, but that, I think, is not a problem." She turned to Ben. "Whilst I understand that you too have love for Jack Carter, and it is your knowledge that has brought you both this far, it is for Michael to continue alone from here. This is more than simply a rescue mission - it has become a quest. A quest that is his destiny and not yours." She smiled, "I see understanding in your eyes. You are a good man, Benjamin Lovecraft. Perhaps you will keep me company during the long hours ahead for Michael?"

Ben's face clouded over, "I'm sorry, but I thought you knew that there is a certain amount of hurry up involved in returning with what these bas... *people* ... want. They gave us twenty-four hours."

Morgana took his hand in her own warm and wrinkled palm. "I know. But here in Avalon, time is not as it is in the outer world. What lies ahead for him will take a day and a night... or maybe longer. But in the outer world it will be but an hour that has passed. Come, walk with me a while, and we can talk. I think that there is much that we can discuss, and perhaps learn from each other." She moved to stand, and Estreya's hand was instantly there under her elbow.

"Thank you, Estreya. You, as always, are my constant and loving support. But you too are weary. Go and rest, child. Benjamin will take me home."

Estreya looked uncertain. "Lady ..."

"Go and rest child, it is my wish. I will be well looked after by this fine man. I promise I will send for you should I need you. Rest, you deserve it, and I have a feeling that I will have need of you refreshed."

Estreya bowed her head to Morgana, and once again gave Ben the warning look that would probably have made Merlin tremble.

Ben took her arm as he cast a glance at Mike's retreating figure, and said a silent prayer. For all of them.

Merlin's expression told Mike everything he needed to know as they walked in silence to the House of the Druids. Whatever lay ahead of him, it was dark and dangerous.

As they entered the low building, men dressed in long robes acknowledged them with reverence, before leaving them alone in the house.

Merlin sat before the blazing fire, and indicated that Mike should sit also. "This is not a situation that has arisen before this day. I have explained to you that it is not our decision to grant you Excalibur. That is so. It is for another to do so, and you shall be given the opportunity to meet her, but you must prove yourself worthy of such an honour. You will know that Arthur, the last Pendragon, fell in battle centuries ago, and sleeps until the land has need of him again. Pendragon is not simply a name, my friend; it is a title, and with it comes a heavy burden of responsibility. There is none of his line to claim Excalibur now, but perhaps it is time for another line to bear the mantle. There is a way, but it is a hard and dangerous path, and one which must be taken before you can go further. The one who can grant you the sword is also the one who can bestow that title. Take heed and remember these words: the last Pendragon was a man of honour and mercy, he knew when to ask for help in the face of danger and death, and he knew the difference between truth and illusion. You have been a warrior in both the physical and the spiritual worlds, but before you can be deemed worthy, you must again be that warrior. Are you ready for such a challenge?"

Mike could feel the pace of his heart increase, and surreal understanding descended on him.

"You mean ...?"

Merlin nodded with a frightening solemnity. "Yes. You must become the Pendragon."

CHAPTER FIFTEEN: THE QUEST BEGINS

Merlin drew nearer to the fire, as if the chill of the Underworld had thrown its cloak around him. He lowered his voice, though the house was empty save for the two of them.

"You must prove yourself to be the Pendragon in a series of trials that will open the door for you. But I must impress upon you, that through that door also lies the path to madness. And perhaps worse. The priestesses will ritually prepare you for the challenge, which you must face alone on the processional path to the stone circle at the top of the Tor."

Mike was pale as he asked quietly, "What challenge?"

"There are four trials, the first three I may not speak of, but the last is the trial of Fire. If you succeed in the first three, the fourth will present itself. Through the flames lies the final ordeal. Only after all trials are successfully completed will you have earned an audience with the one who can grant you Excalibur. If she accepts you as the Pendragon, you will have been granted the sword."

Mike waited in silence, as images and thoughts blew through his brain like fairy dust in the wind. It came down to three things: Beth and Adain, and Jack. He didn't know how, or why, but it seemed they were somehow entwined in his next action. His instinct was to ignore Merlin and Morgana, and go and search for Beth and Adain, but at his core, he knew that he was no match for Nimue. Then a lightning bolt of awareness flashed across his consciousness.

But if he were the Pendragon? With Excalibur? Then, maybe ...

Merlin stared into Mike's eyes as if all of his being was written there. Only a fool would accept this without thought, and Merlin could see no fool in Mike's eyes.

Eventually, Mike said decisively, "I will seek to be the Pendragon."

Merlin nodded his satisfaction, and Mike thought for a single moment that he saw the beginnings of a smile at the corner of his mouth. But it was gone before the thought had time to materialise.

Merlin's tone was one of reverence and concern. "Morgana will be waiting for you. You must be ritually prepared for the challenge. When that is done, then I will accompany you to the foot of the Tor, but from there you will be alone. Whatever you face, I can be of no help to you once your quest has begun."

He reached inside the top of his robe and pulled out a perfect crystal, so clear it could have been frozen from the purest spring water. He took it off and placed it around Mike's neck.

"At least I can give you my blessing and my protection." He lowered his voice. "You may call upon its magic but once. I cannot accompany you; it is all I can do. Now, I will take you to Morgana."

Mike felt the power of the crystal as it settled against his chest, and he felt Merlin's essence combining with it and finding a home somewhere deep within him. And then he accepted the truth of his situation - he may not come back from this one.

He followed Merlin back to Morgana's house. Her fire blazed too, and over it a small, silver cauldron was throwing fragrant steam out into the room. Estreya and a very young priestess named Ayleth stood at the rear of the room, half hidden in shadow, waiting. He wondered what they were waiting for, and then he realised. They were waiting for him.

Morgana took him to the fireplace and bade him kneel before the hearth, as she began a low, musical and rhythmic chant that seemed to have neither beginning nor end. When the chant was over, she beckoned to Estreya and Ayleth to come forward.

"You must be ritually purified and strengthened," she said to Mike, as Estreya poured the fragrant hot water into a bowl and then added water from a jug at the side of the hearth. "An infusion of cleansing and strengthening herbs, and water from the red spring," she said in answer to Mike's unspoken question. "Take off your clothes."

Mike hesitated, and wondered how far this would go. Morgana read him and laughed. The sound of it was soft and possessed the quality of warm syrup, sweet and comforting, and it belied her years. It made him relax, her obvious mirth at his discomfort only served to emphasise its irrelevance.

"Do you balk at this first fence Michael?"

He shook his head and began to disrobe. Morgana bade him kneel before the fire again, and Estreya and Ayleth approached him. The younger of the two was there to assist, and possibly learn, as Estreya began to wash him. He closed his eyes. This was something he hadn't been prepared for.

As Estreya washed him, she gave no sign of any emotion; the only movement in her face was her lips, as they silently prayed. This was an act of reverence and nothing more, and he submitted to it.

Morgana handed him a sheet of linen, and effectively dismissed Estreya and the young woman with the merest inclination of her head. They left with their heads bowed low. Mike wrapped the linen around him, and sat in the chair he had previously occupied. His skin was tingling and hot to the touch.

"Herbs, you say?" he asked Morgana. "I think in the outer world they would be illegal."

Morgana laughed again, "Then what is to come would certainly have you imprisoned. I shall anoint you, and give you a potion which you must drink at the foot of the Tor where your challenge will begin. Are you ready?"

Mike thought he was as close as he could be to ready. He nodded. She bade him lie on his back in front of the hearth.

Morgana opened a tiny silver box which bore the ancient symbol of the Goddess, the pentagram. She dipped her fingers inside and smeared them with the contents. She approached Mike slowly and deliberately, then pressed her fingers to the top of his head, between his eyebrows, and in the centre of his chest, and then washed her hands in the remains of the ritual infusion.

His senses began to swirl and swim around him in a kaleidoscope of colour and sound. His voice was remote and dissociated, as he heard himself say, "What ... the...? Mor-ga-na ..."

Morgana smiled, his journey had begun.

She sat in the chair next to him, watching over him as he journeyed through the barrier, into the nearest reaches of the otherworld, the realm of dreams and visions, where he would prepare for the journey of the hero. Whether he would return as the Pendragon, she knew not. That was up to the Gods.

The sensation of flying had gripped him, and he felt himself rise up from the floor. As he reached the low beams of the ceiling, he felt himself turn over, and he was looking down onto his own inert body. Morgana sat next to him, watching him intently.

Suddenly, that knowledge gave him freedom to soar above the thatched houses of Avalon, until the stone circle at the top of the Tor became as pebbles on a blanket of bright green. He flew higher, and in a wider arc, until he flew over a small island to the north. He descended to take a closer look and enjoy the freedom of his spirit.

The island looked uninhabited, there being no buildings except for what appeared to be an old shepherd's hut, but as he came closer he felt a sharp pull in the middle of his chest, so intense it was painful. The sensation was dragging him down, and it was increasingly difficult to maintain his flight.

It took every ounce of his strength of spirit to rise up again, and return to familiar visions. Avalon was below him. He could see the huts and houses, and he could see the Sacred Well and priestesses at the red spring. He could see the tall stones in a circle on top of the Tor, and suddenly he was over the top of Morgana's house.

He felt the jolt as he returned to his body, and Morgana recognised the change in him as she moved closer. All seemed well, and she relaxed. Just then, Merlin came into the house after a cursory knock and, after satisfying himself that Mike was now only sleeping, he turned to Morgana.

"Get some rest, Lady. There is nothing we can do but watch. He'll be awake soon, and then his real journey will begin. I'll take it from here."

"I'll rest later, when you do, Merlin. In the meantime, would you like some tea?"

Merlin wrinkled his nose in disgust. "Pah! I have no taste for tea, Lady! Tea and the fireside are for the elderly!"

As if on cue, Mike opened his eyes. He tried to get up, but Merlin put a steadying hand on his shoulder.

His voice was low and reassuring, "Take it easy. This is just the beginning."

CHAPTER SIXTEEN: DON'T TURN AROUND

Mike took a shuddering breath, and then gasped, "I know where Beth and Adain are." He described his experience and his vision, finishing with "There was nothing, only an old hut, just one hut."

Morgana sat back in her armchair, "Godney. Nimue has them on the Isle of Godney."

"Then, take me there!"

Morgana cast a significant glance at Merlin, looking for his lead.

Merlin leaned forward in his chair, his elbows resting on his knees, hands clasped together in front of him. "They obviously have some value to Nimue. I know from experience that she does nothing, or takes nothing, without good reason. She clearly knows that you are here, and why. It's Excalibur she wants, and I think that she will hold your wife and daughter as hostages for the sword. I truly believe that they are safe, and will remain so until such time as she uses them to reclaim it."

Mike's distress was obvious, and written into every pore. He sat up and leaned against Morgana's chair, where he found some measure of comfort. She placed a cool hand on his shoulder and locked eyes with Merlin.

"I can try to see them in my mirror," she said, gently.

Mike tried to stand too quickly, and failed. "Scrying, you mean?"

"Yes. If I can see in the mirror that they are safe and well, will you then listen to Merlin's advice?"

Advice! More like a bloody commandment! He gave her a reluctant nod.

Estreya appeared as if from nowhere, gliding like a

ghost to Morgana's side. She was always close by, ready to serve Morgana and her Goddess whenever there was need. There was no air of blind slavery; she clearly served out of love. For both of them.

"Bring my mirror, please Estreya." She returned the girl's warm look with an expression of gratitude and affection. She read Mike's expression of curiosity as Estreya disappeared as silently as she had arrived. "She is my grand-daughter," she said quietly.

Estreya returned only moments later, bearing a bowl carved from pure crystal, as clear as the water with which she filled it. It was difficult to see where crystal ended and water began.

Then she handed Morgana a small vial containing a black liquid. It was a natural dye made from acorns, iron pigments and juices from the Indigo plant, she explained, as she poured it into the bowl. The dense black water reflected the candlelight and, as Morgana passed her hand across the surface, the reflections disappeared.

She sat upright, her hands in her lap, and closed her eyes. Her breathing became deep and settled, and then she opened her eyes and bent over the inky black pool in the crystal. Mike knew better than to speak, or move, or do anything that would break her trance.

Eventually she exhaled deeply and sat upright again. "I see them. They are, as I supposed, on the Isle of Godney, and they are safe and asleep. Nimue has placed her magic over them to keep them that way, creating a magical barrier between them and Avalon, but although I cannot remove the barrier, I can see through it. They are unharmed and unafraid. She is not so much of a monster."

Merlin snorted again, and was quickly quelled by Morgana's steely gaze.

She took both of Mike's hands in hers. "Your daughter is truly remarkable. Even as an infant she has powers beyond what even I imagined. Her soul is ancient, and finds confinement in her infant body difficult. It breaks the confinement and soon it will become worse when she realises that she has magic too. For now, she lies asleep, and yet I felt her reach out to me. She sensed me overlooking them in the ether." She lifted Mike's hands to her temples. "In your semi-altered state, you may be able to see if I place the images for you. Then you will be able to proceed without the distraction of fear for them."

She bent over the crystal bowl again. Mike closed his eyes.

At first, all he could see was the inky blackness of the water. Then, gradually, pictures were forming. He saw the Isle of Godney, standing small and proud in the Severn Sea, like the yolk of a freshly laid egg. He saw the hut again, but this time he could see past the ageing timbers, into the room inside.

Beth lay asleep on what appeared to be a comfortable bed; Adain was curled up in her arms. Both of them looked untroubled in their slumber. Relief flooded him, but, suddenly, from nowhere, a sharp and penetrating pain in his head made him lose contact with Morgana. He balled his fists, and pressed them against his temples. The pain began to subside, and as it did so, he heard a word. Just one word. *Father.*

It was Adain's voice, but it had a mature quality that was far beyond his comprehension. And she had called him 'Father'.

Morgana's care and understanding flew out of the window.

"I need to go there. Now! They are so close; I need to get them away from there! What is *wrong* with you people?!"

Merlin stood and shook his head, and said in an even voice, "No. You have to complete your task now it has begun. And you will be in a better position to bring them home once you are the Pendragon."

Mike was in turmoil. The three people he loved most in the world needed him, but he knew in his heart that Merlin spoke words of wisdom and truth.

He rose onto unsteady feet, "Then we'd better get on with it."

Merlin threw a cream woollen robe to him. He treated Mike to one of his rare smiles. "Put it on. You must face the challenges wearing only virgin wool. I shall take you to the foot of the Tor and there I shall leave you. You must walk the processional way to the top, and on the way you will meet the first three challenges. If you fail just one then the way will be barred to you, and you will go no further. If you pass, then the way will open to you, to the chamber that holds Excalibur, and you will meet the one who will grant you what you seek."

"Who is she?"

When Merlin answered, his voice revealed his respect. "Her name is Erishkigal. She is Queen of the Dragon Clan."

Mike's face was a picture of confusion. "Dragon Clan? As in ...?"

"As in, she is the queen of the dragons. She came here from Sumeria at the beginning of history, and from here she has reigned over the dragons ever since. Excalibur was forged in her fire, and it is she that will decide whether you are worthy of the title 'Pendragon'."

The thought was in his head and out the other side before he could speak it - *'Dragons. Why am I surprised there's dragons?'* He changed tack to Merlin, "I always thought that it was the Lady of the Lake who granted Excalibur."

"And so it was, but since there was no Pendragon to take it, and I was beginning to distrust Nimue, I placed it where I knew it would be safe. It has remained so."

Merlin didn't speak as they approached the Tor from the south west, and this suited Mike as the presence of the hill sought to overwhelm him. He understood without doubt, the meaning of the seven terraces that encircled the Tor in a labyrinth pattern: the ritual way, spiralling to the summit, casting its enchantment over all who trod the sacred path. They passed by the Sacred Well, crossed the field at the foot of the Tor and continued towards two large stones which marked the beginning of the processional way.

Merlin reached inside a pocket in his robe, and brought out a tiny stoneware vial. He uncorked it, and handed it to Mike.

"Drink it all," he said.

Mike was past questions, and in any case, he was going to drink it whatever it was. He tilted it to his lips and swallowed.

Merlin took a step back from him, "I can say only this; do not turn around. Whatever you feel, or hear, behind you, do not turn around. If you turn but once, then what you see will drive you down the path that leads to madness. And remember, you may call on the magic in the crystal once only. Good fortune."

Mike gave no reply as he stepped between the two stones and began the walk through the labyrinth. Merlin settled himself onto the grass beside the stones and closed his eyes. He couldn't accompany Mike, but from the depths of his trance and vision he could watch over him.

After only a few yards, Mike became aware of the potency of the potion he had swallowed. It burned in his stomach first, like a kerosene-fuelled fire, spreading through him, and filling him with the heat of naked flame. He bent over, gasping for air and seeking to cool the inferno, but he instinctively knew that it had to burn out in its own time. It was part of the challenge. He steadied himself and walked on.

With each step he grew quieter inside, and more conscious of how many countless hundreds of feet had walked the path before him. He could feel them, sense their reverence, and it comforted him. Step by step, he descended into a trance-like state, aware of his immediate surroundings but nothing more. Although his feet were bare, each step onto the grassy path seemed to echo inside his brain. He heard each blade of grass buckle and bend beneath his feet, each grain of soil beneath the grass crumble. He could hear the earthworms busily burrowing beneath him.

A huge crow flew overhead, and its cawing boomed inside his mind, so that he covered his ears. It settled on the path ahead of him, head on one side, staring at him with beady black eyes that held more wisdom than seemed good for it.

Without warning it took noisy flight, its cawing call echoing through him and around him, reverberating in his essence. It flapped its wings frantically until a single feather fluttered down to his feet. He stooped to pick it up, and knew instinctively that it was a gift and that he should accept it with gratitude. Without thinking, he pushed it deep into his thick, dark hair. He raised his head to thank the bird, but it was gone.

Another step brought another sensation. Subtle at first, but intensifying with each heartbeat, the vibrations entered through the soles of his feet, rising up into his legs, his torso, his head. A beam of powerful energy rose through him, until it seemed as if his head would explode. The energy burst forth through the top of his head then, in its preordained spear of light, reaching up towards infinity.

Gradually, the intensity of it subsided into a spiral of power that ran up and down his spine, in a dance from the beginning of time. He could feel the earth energy under his feet from the line of power which intersected the Tor, joining sacred sites along its length from St. Michael's Mount in Cornwall to Burrowbridge Mump, then on to the Sacred Well, to the Tor, to Avebury Stone Circle, and onwards - the line of earth energy that had become known as a ley, and had been named the Michael Line. *Appropriate*, he thought.

He let the energy settle in the middle of his chest and walked on. Each step took him deeper into the labyrinth, each breath nearer to his goal. Each breath, slower and deeper. He walked on.

Without realising it, he was on the second tier of the terraces, treading the path that turned back on itself in the true manner of a labyrinth. The buzzing energy in his core softened into a fathomless warmth that suffused his veins, and he allowed the sensation to bathe him, and soothe him. It was a feeling that he didn't have time to savour, as a sudden movement behind him rocketed his senses to alert. Merlin's words of warning echoed in his mind. He must not turn around.

The movement drew closer, and he could feel the heat of another body at his back, creating a sound that made him think of old leather. His mind refused to give it an image, for it would be an image of dread.

His feet had found a mystical rhythm, and he no longer gave conscious thought to the process of walking. Another hundred steps and he rounded the far side of the Tor.

Whatever was stalking him remained close at his back, if anything, it felt still closer. He could hear it breathing; feel its breath on the back of his neck. His instincts were to turn and face it, whatever it was, but he fought the impulse and walked on. So did it.

A hundred more steps and he sensed that the creature had fallen back. He could still feel its presence but the intensity had diminished and he allowed his anxiety level to calm.

There was a sudden change in the atmosphere as his breathing became heavy and laboured. It returned to normal in seconds, leaving Mike with the impression that he had crossed a threshold.

There was a disturbance ahead of him, akin to a heat haze, and he held himself back to watch. The ripples of energy that were creating the effect deepened as they writhed and danced on the turf, becoming green as if contact with the grass had transferred the emerald hue. Something was about to happen, and he knew he was about to face the first of the challenges.

CHAPTER SEVENTEEN: HONOUR AND MERCY

The ripple of energy began to take shape and become dense. Mike could hear the creature behind him find a voice. "Turn around and I'll save you. You can't conquer this challenge - you are unarmed. Turn around and I'll give you a weapon."

Merlin had said nothing about not talking to whatever dogged his footsteps, but he guessed that any interaction with it would be foolish. He ignored it. Ahead of him the energy swirled around the huge form, spiralling upwards to disappear into nothing.

Before him a man rose, tall, powerful, and strong. He was a head taller than Mike and he stood directly in his path, legs astride, shoulders square, and he was wielding an axe. And his whole being was various shades of green.

He wore a suit of armour – *of course he did* – over which he wore a leather tunic and a rich, velvet cloak, all green. His helmet and visor, axe and shield, were also of that colour. Even his beard was the colour of sage. From top to toe, his shades of green varied and blended between the bright green of spring and the deepest, darkest green of winter holly.

He swung the axe in front of him and brandished it between his hands, ready to strike.

"You cannot pass."

Mike took a deep breath and said, in a measured tone, "I must pass."

"Then, you must vanquish me in battle."

"I am unarmed. That's hardly a fair fight; there is no honour in such a battle. I cannot fight you."

"If you are to pass, then you must conquer me. Take

111

up your arms."

Mike was about to repeat his protest, when he saw a short sword and a shield lying on the grass. Apart from a singularly unsuccessful fencing lesson whilst in the RAF, his experience with a sword was less than zero. But he had no choice, it seemed. He bent to pick up the weapon, as his opponent took a step forward.

"To win this battle, you must cut off my head. But first you must answer my question. What is my name? You have three opportunities to speak the correct answer. If you succeed, then also, you may pass."

Mike's thoughts were a kaleidoscope of images from Arthurian legends, finally settling on the obvious and one of his childhood favourites. "You are the Green Knight."

"Wrong!" The axe whistled through the air and Mike only just side-stepped it in time. Before he could breathe, the axe was back in the air, threatening its arc of descent once more. He raised the sword and covered his chest with the shield. Speed was going to be his only chance. The green knight, for that was the only way Mike could think of him, would be slower in his heavy armour.

The axe came crashing down and Mike was quick to fend it off with his shield. He lunged forwards at the middle of the knight's torso, finding only green metal with the end of his blade. The axe was descending again, and again it crashed against his shield, sending him staggering sideways. It came again, and again, and each time he deflected it. He searched for a vulnerable place in the armour but could see none.

Again the crash of blade on shield, but this time Mike only just managed to hold on to the sword. His wrist twisted in the effort, and he swore colourfully.

The voice behind him joined in, "Turn to me, and I will save you. Or you will certainly perish."

Mike ground his teeth, a gesture which brought the old scar on his cheek into high profile, and he shut the voice out of his head. He was quicker this time and as the axe described its arc with deadly force, he brought the sword up underneath the knight's arm and gave it a violent twist. It served to send the knight off balance long enough for Mike to lunge higher with the sword. Still it had no effect as it struck the metal of the knight's green armour.

The axe was in the air again, and the knight was pressing forward, "Do you yield?" he demanded.

"Not a chance in hell!"

"Then speak my name!" was the knight's response.

The mistake was over his tongue, past his teeth, and through his lips before he could stop it. His mind was screaming, *'No! You know that's wrong!'* His voice wouldn't listen and he yelled, "Gawain!"

"Wrong!" The knight pressed further forward, making Mike take a step back. The voice from behind him was there again. "Here, catch!"

Mike was in mid-turn when he saw the axe heading towards his shoulder, fast. His shield was up and made the slightest contact with the sharp blade, just preventing it from slicing through flesh, bone and sinew, severing his limb from his body. As it was, the axe made contact with the side of his upper arm, just beneath the shoulder. The blood was copious and instant. He sucked in his breath, and lunged forward again from behind his shield. This time, the tip of his sword found a small opening in the armour, where the shoulder pieces joined the breastplate, but there hadn't been enough force behind it to do any major damage. Even so, the green armour was slowly beginning to look wet and shiny where his sword had penetrated. The Green Knight was bleeding. And yes, his blood was green.

Mike took strength and hope from the fact that the knight was vulnerable, and rushed towards him, shield raised, sword brandished. He was against the knight's chest and pushing him back, his shield protecting him from the flailing axe. He pushed harder, but the knight didn't fall. The axe was raised again.

"Do you yield?"

Mike raised the sword and shield, and yelled, "This is getting monotonous, now! I said, No! Never!"

"Then, you will die."

Mike felt a sudden heat on his chest, and thought for an instant he'd been mortally wounded, but a far-removed part of his mind recognised the energy of Merlin's crystal. 'My blessing and protection', he had said. *Well, bring on the protection; I'm going to need it!* 'You may call on its magic but once', he'd said. *Was this the time? But if he used it now, would he have greater need of it later?*

He took a quick step back, steadying himself to prevent falling backwards, just as the axe found the centre of his chest, connecting with the crystal instead of his heart. It was as if the axe had made contact with an iron wall, and as it glanced off the crystal Mike could see a large notch in the curve of the blade, ending in a jagged crack from edge to handle. The green axe was damaged.

He knew that it would still be deadly in the knight's hands, but felt a surge of adrenalin hurling him forward again. If he could connect his sword with enough force against the damaged blade, he may have a chance.

There was another clash of axe on shield, as Mike parried the knight's arm. The axe was raised, and Mike could see the vulnerable spot again, but he needed to hit the broken blade. He made a swift decision and raised his sword, not his shield, against the axe. He pushed with his entire body weight against the knight, and they both went sprawling onto the grass.

The axe blade was in two pieces, and Mike took the advantage. He grabbed for the dropped sword, wincing at the pain in his arm that continued to bleed. The Green Knight's armour was heavy, preventing him from rising as swiftly, and Mike was on top of him in an instant, his sword at the knight's throat.

"Do you yield?" Mike challenged him.

"No. You have vanquished me, justly and with honour.

114

Now you must take my head." He turned his head to the side to allow Mike to finish him, and as he did so, his visor fell open, and Mike looked on his face. He withdrew his sword.

"I know who you are," he said.

"Then speak it."

"You are the Green Man, the Holly King of Winter, and the Oak King of Summer. You are the voice on the wind and the face in the leaves. You are the spirit of nature, and I will not harm you."

He put down his sword, and helped the knight to stand. As he did so, the armour began to fall from the knight, revealing his true self. From head to toe, he was covered in foliage from trees and plants of all kinds. His velvet cloak became as meadow grass, and was sprouting colourful flowers of all hues. His eyes and mouth were the only part of his face that wasn't made of leaves. The Green Man indeed.

He seemed to stand even taller without his armour, and the fragrance of evergreen and summer flowers melded into one heady aroma. Mike was puzzled.

"And if I had taken your head?"

"Then you would have failed the challenge, for where is the honour in beheading a man on the ground with no weapon?"

"But you would have taken *my* life."

"If I had wanted to take it I would have done so in the first minute! You have conquered the challenge of mercy and honour. You may pass. And you may take with you the sword and the shield; you will have need of them."

Where the Green Man stood, the grass was growing greener and taller, and flowers were appearing between the green blades. Then everything changed into the rippling haze that had first announced his coming. A whirling vortex of energy was about him, denying Mike further sight of him. Neither could Mike see the path to carry on towards his goal. He had no choice but to wait for it to settle.

"Don't trust him," said the voice behind him. "He waits for you in ambush. He will kill you as soon as you walk on. Look at me, I will show you the way to the top of the Tor without meeting the other challenges."

The hair on the back of Mike's neck and down his arms prickled as they stood to attention. The air between him and whatever stalked him grew cold. The urge to turn threatened to overwhelm his conscious mind, and he felt his body begin to twist and his feet begin to turn. Only the sudden burning in the centre of his chest that emanated from Merlin's crystal severed the compulsion, and brought the warning to the forefront of his mind.

He made no further movement, nor any attempt to speak.

Finally, the whirling energy was gone, and the path lay ahead of him. He paused to tear the hem from his robe and tightly bind the wound on his arm. Then he picked up the sword and shield, and walked on.

The raucous cawing from the crow returned overhead. And once again, the crow began its frantic flapping until several blue-black feathers fell to the ground at Mike's feet. He thanked the bird, this time before retrieving the gift from the ground. Again he absentmindedly pushed them into his hair.

And he walked on.

CHAPTER EIGHTEEN: THE QUESTING BEAST

With each footstep, Mike became more and more distanced from everything, walking mechanically, treading the path of the ancients with a mystical rhythm. He turned his mind inwards, synchronising his heart with the rhythm of his footsteps, the slow, deliberate rhythm of a lone drumbeat. He paced relentlessly onwards, until he realised that he had reached the fourth level of the labyrinth.

At the far edges of his awareness, his stalker grew close again. Mike sensed that it was no longer upright as it dogged his steps; rather it was crawling, then slithering. And it was slithering ever closer. The voice came then, but it was changed in tone and timbre. It was sibilant, hissing at him, its sound sending ice surging in his veins

"Trusssst me. I can sssssave you. Sssseeeker. You cannot trusssst yoursssself, if you wissssh to ssssssurvive."

He was alert in an instant, gripping his sword tighter, but his footsteps never missed a beat in their primeval rhythm.

I will not turn. I will not turn. I will not...

In front of him was an archway of hawthorn, straddling the path ahead. The space between the two uprights of the arch glimmered and shifted, in a curtain of intense energy. He felt the pull in his solar plexus again, drawing him in, pulling him towards his destiny. He tried to halt his steps but found himself moving inexorably, towards what lay beyond.

He reached the archway and could still feel the intense cold coming from his stalker as it writhed towards him.

As he entered the portal his skin tingled and his head felt light and faraway, leaving him with the impression of having stepped into another world. The Tor seemed to have disappeared, and there was no Avalon below him. Instead, he was surrounded by trees in a dense forest that filtered and diminished the light, as it entered through the tangled branches. The floor was covered in pine needles that pierced and stung his bare feet.

The forest was silent, apart from his own movement. No birds sang, no small creatures scurried through the undergrowth. The trees were dense, and the darkness of the forest closed in on him.

The path stretched out ahead of him into the gloom and he instinctively knew that he hadn't entered the portal alone.

I will not turn around.

A sound and movement in the heart of the trees made him halt. He followed the movement with his eyes. Whatever it was, it lived and moved in the dense darkness of the forest. He made a move to follow it, but another glimpse made him falter. He could have sworn he saw the rump and tail of a lion disappear behind a huge pine. Dragons, yes ... well ... maybe ... at a push... after all, this was Avalon, but lions? That, he hadn't been prepared for.

Was this a distraction? Or was it the beginning of the second challenge? He looked straight ahead, and as he did so the serpentine path had disappeared, and as he watched, hawthorn bushes were visibly growing to bar his way. There was no choice but to follow it into the forest.

His stalker followed too, in its slithering, writhing way.

The movement and sound was further away now, so he over-rode caution and went after it. The noise of its movements, cracking branches and tearing undergrowth, informed Mike that it was big. Very big. He gripped his sword ever tighter.

There was another sound now - the noise of barking dogs in the distance. Dogs he knew about, and while they could rip him apart, they evoked less fear than the nameless, shapeless threat in the trees. He moved on, slower now; caution returning to his every pore. It seemed that the barking was coming from the same place as whatever had caused the branches to break.

There was no path through the forest and he had to pick his way through the bracken and the undergrowth, following the sounds ahead. A flicker of movement between two stands of trees made him start. Not a lion. He knew with absolute certainty that what he had seen was in fact the body of a leopard. A bloody big one.

He hadn't seen its head, and for a fragment of time he was grateful for it.

The sudden knowledge that it was doubling back towards him brought with it a slick rivulet of sweat running down his back. What the hell was he doing? He should have gone to the Chapel of St. Mary's with as many loaded guns as he could carry and killed the bastards that held Jack. He wasn't up to this. It wasn't even his world. And now, because he had come here on this crazy mission, Beth and Adain were also in danger. He'd been convinced he could sort it all out. He was astounded by his own arrogance - he'd been a jerk.

Without thought or acknowledgement he touched Merlin's crystal, and without thought, but with a sudden, deep acknowledgement his courage returned. It wasn't a case of '*he couldn't do this*', it had to be '*he could and would do it*'.

He raised his sword and followed the noise deeper into the forest.

The sound of barking dogs grew nearer. What was this? Were there two challenges here? A pack of angry dogs, as well as the thing he'd half seen through the trees?

The ever present voice behind him gave emphasis to his dilemma. It laughed derisively.

His attention was brought back with a jolt to what lay ahead. The beast had come up on him from his left flank, and now stood, unmasked by trees, directly in front of him.

119

Mike swallowed hard, and his saliva stuck in his constricted throat. His eyes were wide, but his mind was slower in comprehension of the beast. His synapses fired at an alarming rate as he flipped through his dusty mental files to find the answer.

He was looking at a beast the size of an elephant. Its head, which was three times the size of his own, was that of a King Cobra, its hood fully extended. The torso was indeed that of a giant leopard and it ended in the rump of a lion. Recognition emerged from the dusty files as the beast drew back its head and lunged at Mike, mouth open, enormous fangs bared, its forked and barbed tongue flicking in and out as its mouth dripped venom. Bizarrely, the noise of barking dogs seemed to be coming from its stomach.

It was the Questing Beast.

Mike thought his heart was going to stop as it missed at least three beats from its regular rhythm. He flung himself sideways, as the beast followed suit in a single bound.

What little he knew about the Questing Beast from his familiarity with the Arthurian legends shot through his brain in milliseconds.

The monster was said always to appear where there had been an incestuous relationship, and it was well known that Morgana had coupled with her brother, Arthur, at the Beltane Fires; both of them unaware that the other was their sibling. The union had been the result of the meddling by the then-Lady of Avalon, in an effort to secure the safety and future of Avalon and the Old Religion. Morgana had given birth to Mordred as a result of their union, and the fate of Arthur was sealed. As was the fate of Morgana.

One of Arthur's knights, Sir Pellinore, had spent his life in search of the Questing Beast, vowing to rid the land of it, but when one day he had come upon it lying wounded, he had cared for it and set it free. Mike doubted it was going to be that easy for him. And in any case, he had passed the challenge of honour and mercy. This time he knew he would have to kill it. He just didn't know how.

Thought processes that flashed through him in a heartbeat dissolved instantly as the beast made another lunge. Mike was all too aware that he couldn't turn around, and knew that whatever followed him was too close for comfort. He daren't fall back and he couldn't go forward, so he hurled himself sideways, wrenching his titanium knee joint and sending shards of red hot pain into his whole body as he crashed into a tree. The snake neck of the beast whirled around after him, and lunged at his neck, its fangs ripping a long tear in his robe, but his flesh remained intact.

Whether he would have need of it later or not, now was the time to call on Merlin's magic. Without it he was facing death, of that he had no doubt. He grasped the crystal, and his voice echoed through the forest. He felt the heat of the crystal, and he heard the power in his voice.

"I call upon the magic of the Merlin of Britain. Come to my aid!"

He had expected lightning bolts, crashes of thunder, or, at the very least, a shower of sparks. None of which appeared. Not even a feeble puff of smoke. Instead, he felt a sudden breeze encircle him and pick him up, as if he'd been Dorothy bound for Oz. It lifted him, and deposited him squarely onto the beast's back.

There was no time for thought. He flung himself at its neck and dropped his shield onto the ground below. With his free arm tight around its throat, preventing it from turning its head, he drove his sword straight down through its neck and out the other side.

The beast threw itself from left to right in an effort to dislodge him, but it didn't fall. Mike tried to pull his sword free, but the force of his blow had it firmly lodged. The Questing Beast was hissing, raging and squirming, as it tried desperately to turn its head, with its deadly fangs coated in venom and ready to strike. Mike hung on, horrified at what may happen if he once relaxed his iron grip. Pulling the sword free with one hand took all his strength, but it came out with a squelching sound that sickened him. The beast was screaming in agony now, and Mike was determined to finish it with the second strike. He aimed a little higher this time, and with everything he had left, he brought the sword down again. This time, the Questing Beast gave a terrible cry and took a halting step forwards, and then it fell onto its side, its agony over.

In Avalon, Morgana heard the beast's dying screams in her mind, felt its death in her heart. A single tear slid down her face, and dripped onto her folded hands, and she knew that her penance was over. Her Questing Beast was slain by the Would-Be-Pendragon. She offered a prayer of thanks and a plea for his safe-keeping. For surely he would have need of it.

Mike fell from the beast's back and landed awkwardly on his damaged leg, retching at the sudden rainbow of colours that accompanied the searing pain.

He lay in a heap at the dead beast's side, breathless and with unstoppable tears that meandered through the dirt on his face, leaving white rivers in the grime. He didn't know who the tears were for. Not for himself, but maybe for all of them.

He tried to stand, but the pain that shot through his leg, and into his body, brought him back to his knees. The laughter from behind had become manic, and it took all his strength not to turn around and lash out at whatever had given voice to it.

Ahead of him, at the far side of the forest, a light was shining. He could see that the trees were thinner there and he knew it was the direction that he should take. The labyrinthine path had long since disappeared, leaving only his instincts to guide him. He was exhausted, mentally, physically, and emotionally, but he dragged himself to his feet again. Leaning against a tree, he picked up his sword and hacked a forked branch from it, cutting the forks to a short length to form a make-shift crutch. He swore loudly, and with feeling, as the memories of trying to walk again after the crash washed over him. He'd vowed on the day he had parted company with his crutch that he would never have need of one again.

He didn't know if he could go further, but he had to. For Beth. For Adain. And for Jack.

He bent to retrieve his sword and shield, but they were nowhere to be seen. Taken from him in the same manner as they had been gifted.

CHAPTER NINETEEN: NIMUE

On the Isle of Godney, Beth was awake.

She kept her body still and her eyes closed. Her arms closed in tighter around Adain, and she listened to her regular, breathing. Addie was in a deep sleep. She stroked the child's cheek, marvelling at its softness, and then she bent over her and kissed her gently on the cheek. "Stay asleep Addie, and dream sweet dreams while I try and find a way out of here."

She needed to think, and whilst their captor believed them to be asleep, they would have more opportunity to try to escape. She knew that they were on a small island, little more than a mound in the middle of the waters surrounding Avalon. She may be able to swim for it, but Adain would have to be carried and kept safe in the process. She knew she wasn't up to that, so she cancelled it from her options.

Rowan - for that is who she still believed held them - was tall and slender, but Beth had no doubt of her strength, and that was without the obvious magical abilities. She was certain that the priestess must have used magic to make them both fall asleep in that way. She briefly considered the possibility of overpowering her, but conceded that it would be too risky.

She sensed that they were in no danger. Yet. Rowan had made them safe, comfortable and warm, a log fire burned in the small hearth and there was bread and fruit on a small table. Beth lay still and strained to hear any movement within the small hut, or from outside. There was no sound from inside or out.

She tentatively took her arm from around Adain and laid her gently against the soft pillow, covering her with the woollen blanket that had been placed over them both. Adain didn't stir. Beth checked her breathing again, and felt her cheek and forehead with the back of her hand. She was warm, and her deep breathing was regular and untroubled. Satisfied, she straightened up and rose slowly from the bed, desperate not disturb even a mote of dust that may alert the priestess to her waking.

She opened the door slowly and carefully, and was surprised to see only darkness outside. There was no window in the hut and she hadn't realised it was night.

It was at this time that Nimue had walked into Avalon, having taken the barge that had brought them to Godney. She made straight for Morgana's house.

As she approached, two Druids noticed her; they could hardly fail with her tall willowy stance, and her cascade of red wavy hair, left free of binding , that reached half way down her back. She exuded power and magic, but still they made to prevent her from going further. They were no match for Nimue with all of Merlin's magic, and were soon lying on the ground, unconscious.

Estreya saw her next and hurried to Morgana's side.

"Lady, Nimue is here. She is coming this way."

Before Morgana could reply, Nimue was in the door and standing before her.

Estreya's hand was quickly under Morgana's elbow as she stood straight, defiant, eyes blazing at Nimue.

"You have the nerve to return here?" she demanded.

Nimue smiled with derision at her, leaving Morgana in no doubt as to her malice.

"I see time has not mellowed you, Morgana. You are still bitter and unforgiving. We both know that it is I who should be the next Lady of Avalon. I have served well as the Lady of the Lake, now it is my turn. You shall have your infant protégé, and she shall become your successor, but first I have come for Excalibur. I am still the Lady of the Lake and I demand its return. Only then shall I give you the child."

"You forget yourself, Nimue, Excalibur is not yours to take. You sacrificed that honour when you broke with Avalon to pursue your own ends. There is a place in the world for all faiths, and while the New Religion has no tolerance for the Old, we must show them that followers of the Old Religion present no threat to them, and that we can exist in harmony. Avalon is not about one person alone, it is a sacred charge. And so is Excalibur."

Nimue waved her arm dismissively, "Well, that may be your opinion. I, on the other hand, will not tolerate the usurping of the Gods and Goddesses of our land. It's very simple. The child for the sword."

"Nimue, since you have been asleep, over the many centuries, the intolerance has grown and our faith has all but been eradicated, driven underground, at one time made illegal even and its followers put to death. In the outer world, the love of the Goddess is only just re-emerging into a world that is ready to greet her and serve her again. Avalon removed itself from that world in an effort to keep the love and loyalty to the Goddess alive. You know that I cannot agree to your demand. Please, Nimue, don't turn this into a battle."

"*A battle?* My dear Morgana, have you not looked into the mirror recently? You have grown old and frail, and no doubt your magic has faded with your beauty. It would be no battle."

Morgana's eyes blazed with dragon fire but she dare do nothing that would endanger Adain. She had seen that the child and her mother were safe, and she had also seen the magic barrier, like a dome of electricity, which contained and imprisoned the two on Godney. Nimue's words were harsh, but they contained an element of truth - her magic had faded. There was a sudden leap of a flame in her chest, and her eyes reflected its glow. Or perhaps not.

Nimue's eye roved over Morgana's home, and she suddenly stiffened.

"Merlin. He's alive? He's here?" For a fraction of a

second there was a flicker of hesitation and doubt, but it vanished as quickly as it had appeared. She was once again, Nimue, the Lady of the Lake.

Morgana saw her opportunity to take the upper hand. Merlin would always be Nimue's weakness and she had no shame in capitalising on it, especially while Merlin was locked safe in deep meditation and vision, watching over Mike on the Tor.

"Yes, Nimue, he is here. But perhaps your magic is not as powerful as you would like to believe if you are only just realising that your death blast failed in its task. I'm surprised that you didn't sense his living, sleeping breath from your own imprisonment in slumber. Can it be that he has no love for you anymore? Perhaps his magic is more powerful, and he has kept himself hidden from you. Why do you think that would possibly be?"

Nimue's face clouded and her eyes darkened dangerously, "I see you still have a viperous tongue, old woman! I am the love of his life and he will come to me when I call."

"Really? Where is he, I wonder? He is here, and by now the whole of Avalon knows of your presence. He doesn't seem to be in a great hurry to come to your side." Morgana knew that she didn't dare to provoke her too far and precipitate the inevitable. Nimue was intent on war.

Nimue's words were laced with venom. "Be assured, dear Lady of Avalon, I will possess Excalibur once more, if you wish to see the child alive. I will return after the passing of another night and I will expect to receive what is rightfully mine. Once I have Excalibur, I will lift the curse on Godney, and you can have your feeble infant."

She gave Morgana no further opportunity to rattle her, she needed to be in control. She turned on her heel and left.

No-one stood in her way, all taking their lead from Morgana, whose expression as she stood in her doorway, said, 'Let her go. For now.'

CHAPTER TWENTY: TRUTH AND ILLUSION

The pain in Mike's leg was excruciating but he pushed on towards the light at the edge of the forest. His companion crow was expected and didn't disappoint him. It circled overhead, cawing and gliding on the wind. The make-shift crutch was doing its job and he leaned heavily on it. Crow flapped it wings and the feather drifted down towards him. He had no idea why he would have need of the feathers but his instinct told him that they would be important to his success. He gathered it up and, without any other refuge for it, he pushed it into his hair with the others.

His progress was slow as he hobbled towards the patch of light. He had no idea how much time had elapsed in facing the first two challenges, but the light encouraged him. He was oblivious to the notion of Faerie light, and how it played its tricks.

At the foot of the Tor night had fallen, and Merlin remained in his trance vigil. He hadn't moved, nor blinked, nor given any conscious thought since first the trance was upon him. He had seen Mike defeat the Green Knight and recognise him in truth as the Green Man. He had seen his crystal go to Mike's aid against the Questing Beast. And now, the third challenge lay ahead of him, upon which success or failure to gain an audience with Erishkigal rested. Merlin knew that the slightest interference from him would result in Mike's failure, so he waited, and he watched.

A voice behind him, seductive and warm, brought Mike back to an awareness of his stalker.

"Rest a while, Seeker. You are injured and exhausted. No good will come of facing the next challenge without rest. Wisdom must take precedence over valour now. Rest with me, and gather your strength." The voice was female, husky and deep, with a hypnotic quality. He felt himself begin to relax, his shoulders dropped, and the knotted muscles in his neck eased their hold on sinews that were as taut as piano strings.

He heard her close behind him, felt her warm breath on the back of his neck again, and he smelled her musky perfume. Suddenly, all he wanted was to lie down on the warm forest floor with her, listening to the sound of the voice that had found entry into his mind.

He felt his knees and hips begin to accept the invitation, ready to lower him to the ground. It seemed as if he could listen to the voice forever. He was tired. More tired than he could ever remember. He felt his eyelids becoming heavy, heard the voice behind him becoming muffled and distant.

Felt himself begin to turn around.

He had made a half turn, and then, as he heard her sharp intake of breath, he turned his head towards the sound.

The spell was broken by the harsh and raucous cawing of Crow overhead. He faltered and blinked his eyes, breaking through the hypnotic hold she had on his mind. Beads of perspiration broke on his forehead as Merlin's dire warning resounded inside his head.

I will not turn around. I will not.

His stalker gave a loud shriek of frustration, which only served to make Mike smile. But he was only too well aware of how close he had come to his downfall. He took a deep breath, and limped on his crutch towards the rectangle of light.

After several minutes he paused, and frowned in puzzlement. It didn't matter how many painful steps he took, the light just didn't seem any closer. Was this where he was meant to be headed? Was there any other way out of the forest? He looked to left and right, and only saw dense trees and undergrowth. He knew he couldn't turn around, and so the only way forward had to be towards the rectangle of light.

He limped on towards it.

Gradually it seemed nearer, and larger. As he drew ever closer, he could see that in fact it was two doorways, side by side, and giving forth the light that suddenly had adopted an eerie quality. The forest appeared denser and deeper on either side. The doorways were the only path out.

He approached the doorways with caution, instinct telling him that he must choose which doorway to enter and that he would only get one shot at it. He shook his head, suddenly feeling as if he was a participant in some cheesy game show, and at any minute a simpering host would ask him to choose the door to fame and fortune, or the one that would take him to an alley at the back of the TV studio. He sighed. This was no game, but the choice had to be made.

As he approached, the light that emanated from the doorways began to shimmer and shift. As it settled again, Mike could see the landscape on the other side.

The scenery behind the left hand door was the serpentine path up to the top of the Tor. There didn't appear to be any obstacles in the way. Through the right hand door, it was dark, and the path appeared to disappear into rocky crevices.

An idea was forming in the far recesses of his mind but hadn't quite made it to conscious thought. Something Merlin had said.

He sat down in front of the doorways to think. The obvious choice was the clear path to the stone circle. But this was a challenge, and where would be the challenge in simply stepping through the door that led to his goal? But only a fool would willingly step into darkness and danger. If he took the easy route, did that mean he would fail the challenge? If he took the dangerous route, would that make him a fool?

Merlin's words were still trying to force their way to the front of his mind. He thought about the previous challenges. His opposition then had been obvious. He had passed the challenge of honour and mercy, and ... and that was it!

Merlin had said quite deliberately - and laboured the point that he should remember his words - that the last Pendragon, Arthur, had been a man of honour and mercy. That he had known when to ask for help when faced with death, and that he could tell the difference between truth and illusion. The first challenge had been to test his honour and his mercy in sparing the Green Man, the second test had prompted him to use Merlin's crystal as the Questing Beast was about to deliver his death. He had known when to ask for help. Logically, that meant that this challenge was about truth and illusion.

Years previously, as he had lain in a hospital bed recovering from the devastating helicopter crash, he had read avidly, looking for answers about life and death. Now he remembered reading words from the Indian guru, Sai Baba:- *'Do not be misled by what you see around you, or be influenced by what you see. You live in a world which is a playground of illusion, full of false paths, false values and false ideals. But you are not part of that world.'*

Could it be that simple? That this was all illusion? That either doorway would lead him to the summit of the Tor? Or were *all* of the challenges illusory? Was he still unconscious in Morgana's house? Was he even there at all? He groaned, continuing to explore these thoughts would drive him mad.

One thing he did know – he was getting severely fed up with it all.

It was all well and good for them to talk of destiny, his and Adain's. And that was the point. It was *his* destiny, no-one else's, and *he* alone would decide it. As for Addie, she was still a baby, and if any decisions were going to be made on her behalf, it would be him and Beth making them, and no-one else.

Sai Baba's words '... *not of this world.*' ran amok in his head. He was definitely not of this world, so why should he be concerned with it? He answered his own question.

Because without co-operation from this world, Jack was going to die in his own.

He stood up and faced the doorways.

If this was illusion, had *he* created it? In searching for a way out of the forest, had he created the illusion of a way out? In creating that, had his mind embellished the illusion into two doorways because of his fears or insecurity?

One truth was irrefutable, he had to move forwards. He had to go through one of the doorways. This was a quest, and quests demanded action, not sitting around contemplating the universe, or even his navel. He was no philosopher, not even an armchair one. He was over-thinking it.

The moment that he acknowledged the thought, the words of one of his all-time heroes, and unlikely philosopher, echoed through him. '*Imagine there's no heaven, it's easy if you try. No hell below us, above us only sky.*' He had also said that *reality left a lot to the imagination.* Thank you, John Lennon.

He grinned. He knew.

Both doors were indeed self-created illusions. If he had created them, he could recreate them. He stepped through the right hand door, which led to darkness and danger.

Just for the hell of it.

CHAPTER TWENTY ONE: HERE BE DRAGONS!

As he stepped through the doorway the veil of illusion vanished, and before him was the processional path to the stone circle.

He knew what to expect here: Merlin had said that the final challenge was of Fire.

As he approached the tall stones he felt, deep within, that he was treading on sacred ground, and his mind-set shifted accordingly. He walked forwards with a sense of reverence.

This was no illusion; it had been constructed by physical hands from the earth's own physical materials. The entrance was obvious, as he stood before two upright stones with a horizontal lintel. Another doorway. He made a move towards it, but halted before his steps could take him through.

Out of the west, a whirring noise assailed his ears. It was accompanied by the sounds of flapping, leathery wings. And it was getting hot.

The dragon appeared from nowhere, belching flames and heat, both directed downwards. As it flew over the stone circle, white hot, searing flames hit the ground in front of each stone, creating its own circle of fire. The inner perimeter of the stone circle was engulfed in Dragon Fire.

Once more his mind travelled back to in his hospital bed, where he had learned a technique to take him beyond his pain. He could do it again.

The conflagration was a roaring wall of fire and searing heat. He steadied himself, controlled his breathing, opened his mind, and stepped into the inferno.

The fire raged around him, flames licking at his woollen robe, his feet, his skin, his hair. His mind remained firm and steady, his breathing barely perceptible, his belief, concrete.

He would become the Pendragon.

He stepped through the fire, ignoring everything that was outside his mental control. His mind didn't acknowledge the flames, accepting them as part of the stone circle. At the epicentre of the inferno, the stone altar was in the eye of the firestorm, and no flames reached it. He stepped reverently and solemnly towards it, towards the ancient altar, on which rested a plain silver chalice.

The Grail? The end of the quest? His goal?

Suddenly all around him stilled, and as the veil lifted, he saw that it was night. How long had he taken on this quest? How much time had he wasted while Jack's very life hung in the balance? But there was no hurrying now. Something else was happening to him.

It started in the soles of his feet, a tingling sensation similar to his experience as he stepped between the marker stones at the foot of the Tor. But more intense, more far-reaching.

It travelled along the now-familiar path of his spine, activating and uplifting the energy centres as it spiralled, serpent-like, from the base of his spine, right up through the top of his head, where it found its release.

The energy brokered by the Tor had its source in the divine and, in a blinding flash of revelation, one face was before him. Beth. In that moment in time, he understood. He understood her passion for her Goddess, for now he had felt her too.

And he understood that whilst every land had its faiths and deities, Old, New, East, and West - all spirituality had but one source. And the source was both God and Goddess, for how can one be without the other. To be otherwise would defy all laws of nature.

The Christ had indeed been the saviour of his people,

but the saviour of Albion had a feminine hand ... The Goddess.

He fell to his knees, unaware that tears were streaming down his face but knowing that he would never be the same again. He would be forever transformed by the love he had felt. And he ached for Beth, to tell her, to share with her what she already embraced.

He had come to Avalon for one reason only. To obtain what the Inquisition demanded for Jack's life. And he hadn't cared how he would come by it. He had followed the instructions of Merlin and Morgana like an empty headed child, bent only on the prize. But he hadn't bargained for the journey. Or its effect on him. He had agreed to 'become' the Pendragon, because that was what was required to obtain his goal. He had no idea of what that meant.

Now he did.

The Pendragon may be a title, but it was also a sacred duty, a duty to honour and serve the Goddess, to become one with the land and learn its secrets and rhythms, and to honour it. Not as a God, but as the result of the union between God and Goddess. The God and the Great Mother. If he was to accept the title, Pendragon, he would have to accept the duty that accompanied it. For Avalon. For Beth. For himself. And now, with this sudden understanding, he knew it would be for Adain too.

He saw her destiny with different eyes. They said she would unite Avalon with the outer world, bring healing between Pagan and Christian, just as the last Pendragon had. The realisation brought another understanding. He may, or may not, come to bear the title' Pendragon', but if he did - if he was deemed worthy - it would be in trust for the one who would ultimately claim it. Adain.

Until that time, he would swear to protect Avalon in any way he could, given the limitations of his humanity.

Tears still blinded him as he stood to face the ancient altar, not just stone any longer but something deeper, something mystical. The silver chalice glinted in the light of the rising moon, throwing its reflections into the shadows on the ground, calling him, beckoning to him. Was he meant to drink from it? Would it be sacrilege?

There was only one way to find out. He picked it up and raised it to his lips. The feeling in his chest threatened to explode through his ribcage, expanding, growing, consuming. In truth, this was a sacred union. The crystal water of the Sacred Well felt like a blessing, and he drained the chalice and replaced it lovingly on the altar. The moment that he did so, the flames died away, leaving only undamaged blades of grass.

The rumble was distant at first, coming from deep within the conical hill. The ground moved under his feet. The rumbling grew louder, and he took an instinctive step sideways. Before his feet were firm on new ground, there was the sound of tearing turf as the ground tore apart, revealing a flight of stone steps that disappeared into darkness.

Mike took a tentative step forward and began to descend the cold, stone stairway, towards the belly of the Tor.

The stairway was dark, and as he descended the roughly-hewn steps, towards the ever-increasing blackness, the fleeting impression of a tomb was quickly dismissed. He was close now, close to more than he had ever dreamed of when he came to Avalon. Then, all he had wanted was to go back to the bastard from the Inquisition and get Jack the hell out of there. Many times since then he wished he'd just shot the Prefect and his henchmen. If he'd thought for one minute that he'd have been able to get Jack out in one piece by shooting his way through, he'd have done it in a heartbeat. But the image of Alessio's hand on the huge wheel that threatened to break Jack's spine with the merest tug, wouldn't leave him.

And he thanked the Goddess for it, because without that instinct he would never have understood. Now, the quest for Excalibur was more than stupid challenges set by unknown hands. Now it was a trial of his worthiness and his honour. He swallowed hard, and prayed he had proved himself.

As he neared the foot of the steps he could see a soft orange glow. It appeared to come from an opening out of the tunnel at the foot of the stone steps.

He approached it with caution and no small amount of respect.

The tunnel did indeed open out into a huge cavern. Mike looked up and could only just make out the shadows on the ceiling, so high was it. The entire chamber was bathed in the flickering light of amber, orange, and red shades of fire. All of which emanated from the enormous, sleeping dragon which lay directly in front of him.

CHAPTER TWENTY TWO:
ERISHKIGAL

The Queen of the Dragon Clan lay before him, curled upon herself in the way of a sleeping cat, her snout buried against her haunches. But Mike knew only too well that this was no sleeping mog.

The source of the flickering light was immediately apparent, as was the rumbling. With each exhalation, small tongues of flame issued from her nostrils, accompanied by the deep, regular rumble. The old girl was snoring.

Mike grinned.

He stepped over her outstretched barbed tail to get a better look at her. Mistake number one.

"Well, I'll be damned! Just look at *you*!"

Erishkigal was covered in large, leathery scales, and she was a myriad of shimmers and colours, like petrol on water. She was amazingly beautiful and Mike was momentarily lost in her awesomeness. Mistake number two.

She shifted restlessly, and snorted a larger tongue of flame.

Mike took a step back, and mistake number one reared up and hit him on the backside. Literally. She gave an annoyed flick of her tail and swiped him clean off his feet. He landed awkwardly and ignominiously on his side, and the pain that ensued made him swear, graphically. He hoped Erishkigal was unfamiliar with slurs on parentage.

Mistake number two followed hard on the heels of its predecessor, as Mike's lost concentration made him miss the lifting of her head and the opening of the deepest amber eyes.

And then she spoke to him.

"Who are you? And what do you want?" She didn't wait for his breathless reply. "Ah. I see. It is the sword you seek. But you don't look like a king, and while you wear the dress of a druid, you aren't a druid."

She bent her neck forwards and sniffed the air, and Mike was caught in the middle of a huge gust of wind.

"You are from the outer world! I can smell it all over you!" She wrinkled the scaly nostrils in distaste.

Mike responded out of instinct and without the reverence he had previously felt. "*Hey!* I don't know about here, but in my world, we treat our guests with some measure of courtesy!"

"Yes. I know. You give them ... tea. And you are *not* a guest. You are an *intruder!*" She adopted the expression of a grumpy old lady, woken from her afternoon nap.

Mike took another step closer.

"Look ... *Your Majesty* ... I have had ... a *really* bad day. And it isn't over yet! So, I'll ask you nicely to give me the sword. The life of a dear friend ... one who is like a brother ... depends upon it."

"Are you done whining? I'm tired."

"Well, if it's tired you want, take a look at me!" He held his arms out from his sides. "Look at me! I'm injured, I'm filthy, and *tired* doesn't cover it. I have come to claim Excalibur. I have been sent here by Merlin of Britain!"

The Dragon Queen raised herself on her haunches and Mike gasped at the size of her. He stood six feet two in his socks, and Erishkigal was three times his height without standing. He swallowed hard and retreated four steps backwards.

"Are you afraid of me?" she snorted.

Mike chose to ignore the question, and its implication.

"Will you give Excalibur to me?"

She tossed her head, "Merlin of Britain, you say? Hm, nevertheless, I am disinclined to do so."

Mike had had it. "You know what? Forget it! I know it's here, and I'll find it and take it. But I promise you this,

I *will* return it. And thanks for nothing!"

If a dragon could smile, Erishkigal gave a pretty damn good impression of it. She shifted her weight back onto her belly and Mike got a fleeting glance of something that glinted underneath her.

She was sitting on Excalibur.

Something inside him snapped. In fact it twanged like a broken guitar string.

"I've walked your Dragon Path of Dreams, and I've drunk ... hell if I know *what* I've drunk! I've fought the Green Knight and killed the Questing Beast! And I *really* don't want to know what was following me! I've walked through fire ..." He paused as emotion filled him at the next thought. He dropped his voice, "I've felt the Goddess move through me," he looked up, his voice strong again, "And now I'm here, under the Tor, talking to a dragon! Forgive me if I seem tetchy! But I have already told you, there is one whose life depends upon this. Merlin asked me if one man's life is worth such a high price. I say, yes, it is! It's about honour and mercy, and I'm here asking for help - and if you're an illusion, there must have been some heavy crap in that drink! What is the point of lying there on top of the sword, if you won't allow it to make a difference?"

Erishkigal put her head on one side and breathed out a tongue of flame. "I know what you have accomplished, you wear the tokens."

Mike wasn't in the mood for riddles, "*Tokens?*"

"You have received a token for each challenge completed. My friend Crow has given them to you."

Mike put a hand to his hair and smiled as he touched the feathers.

Erishkigal continued, "Excalibur is in my care until the Pendragon comes again to claim it."

"Arthur is gone! But you know that. The last Pendragon is 'asleep', if that's how you want to look at it! I have done *everything* that I was asked to do. I *am* the

Pendragon!" A sudden moment of clarity in the madness brought a terrifying calm. He relaxed, drew himself up to his full height, and spoke with measured authority and power. "I am the Pendragon, and I come to claim Excalibur."

Erishkigal turned her deep amber eyes directly onto his face.

"Why didn't you say so?"

Mike couldn't help it, the laugh was deep and loud and out of his mouth before he could stop it.

"You find it amusing, Pendragon?"

Mike sobered, "No. I apologise. This is ... new to me."

"Clearly." She shifted her bulk and rose onto her legs, revealing Excalibur beneath her. "If you are to become Pendragon, you must claim Excalibur and wear the marks. Take the sword, Pendragon."

Excalibur gleamed in the warm light, sending reflections skittering around the cave, proclaiming its power and sovereignty. He had expected the sword to be encrusted with jewels at the hilt, but Excalibur needed no such ornament. Its simplicity and purity spoke for itself. Mike bent forwards and pulled the sword towards him, entranced by the musical sound it made as its blade slid across stone. He hesitated, was this too easy?

Erishkigal read him, "Pick up Excalibur, Pendragon. It will only come to you if you are truly worthy."

Another test?

He grasped the hilt firmly and stood upright, brandishing Excalibur, seemingly feather-light in his hand, high above his head. He was unprepared for the sensations that filled him.

Images of battles fought and won, reflections in a mirror of acts of chivalry and mercy filled his head, and finally, he was one with the passing of the last Pendragon and felt his last breath. He gasped and bent forwards, disorientated and depleted. He was done.

Erishkigal opened her leathery wings to their full span

and stood erect, towering over him. She flapped her leathery wings, creating a whirlwind of air that surrounded him. She was applauding the new Pendragon.

She settled again and leaned in towards him. "You are worthy of the title Pendragon, which I bestow upon you. Now, you must bear the marks." Seeing his expression change, she allowed him no time for protest as he was already half way back down the Tor in his head.

She said, "This place is not a place, this time is not a time; it exists between the worlds and beyond. Worry not, Pendragon, you must tarry here to receive the marks before departing. Come closer."

Mike had no fear of her, and approached her confidently.

"Put down the sword and bare your forearms."

Mike obeyed her without fear. Whatever this was, it would seal the deal.

Erishkigal appeared to inhale deeply, and then exhaled long and slow, a blinding flame of white fire, directly onto Mike's arms.

The pain was intense as the searing burn played momentarily over his arms, and just when he thought he was going to pass out, Erishkigal backed away, her flame dying away to a tiny puff of steam.

He fell to his knees, head bowed, perspiration dripping from his face, his heart pounding. He looked at his arms, expecting seared and withered flesh.

There was no trace of burned skin or flesh; instead, his forearms bore a brand. The mark of the Pendragon. On each forearm a dragon reached from his wrist to his elbow, serpentine, black and wonderful.

He couldn't speak, emotion was the victor. And he allowed himself the luxury of a single tear.

The Queen of the Dragon Clan did something extraordinary then. She bowed to him.

"The loyalty of the Dragon Clan is yours, Pendragon." Her voice changed in tone then, lifted, lighter. "Behind you." She nodded with her beautiful, scaly head, towards the rear of the cave. And he knew it would be safe now to turn around.

There was a rocky ledge on which stood the plain silver chalice that had been on the ancient altar in the stone circle.

"Drink it all," she said. "It will heal the burns and take away the pain."

The chalice appeared to contain only water, but as he swallowed, he felt it in every pore of his body, warming, cooling, soothing, energising ... healing. He lifted his head and looked into the amber eyes.

"Thank you, Your Majesty." This time there was no hint of sarcasm in his voice as he addressed her in that way.

She bowed her head briefly in acknowledgement.

Curiosity is a strange beast and it overtook his speech. "How many of you are there? If you don't mind me asking."

Erishkigal appeared to ponder the question. "In the outer world, we are all but extinct, hunted and killed millennia ago by humans that had no understanding of our ways. And the ones of my clan that remain there lie deep in the hills of your landscape. Your ancestors knew of their presence and called such places, the Dragon's Back, Dragon Ridge and such like. Your Malvern Hills, the mountains of Snowdonia, the Pennine range and the mountains of Scotland, all are home to my clan. If you look with the right eyes you can see them. In this world, we are still few in number but we are free to fly where we will. Now, are you refreshed?"

Mike nodded to her and picked up Excalibur. He held the sword upright in front of him in a salute to The Queen of the Dragon Clan.

"Your journey back down the Tor will be unhindered. Merlin of Britain awaits you below. He has not moved since the moment you stepped onto the processional path.

Good fortune, Pendragon, we will meet again."

Mike nodded. "I will return Excalibur as I promised."

"It does not belong in the outer world, but it will always be here, waiting for you should you ever have need of it. Excalibur is at your command, but it belongs in Avalon."

Mike retraced his footsteps up the stone stairs, which strangely seemed to go on for much longer than when he had descended. Eventually, he reached the top and stepped out into the stone circle.

Dawn was breaking, and the mist lay heavy on the fields and on the waters that surrounded Avalon, giving the impression that the top of the Tor was an island in the mist. The serpentine path around the Tor lay veiled before him, but he lingered in the stone circle. He was unsure of ritual or traditions, but he knew that before he left, there was something he had to do.

He knelt before the stone altar and laid Excalibur on it. He bowed his head and closed his eyes. His voice was stilled but he spoke with his heart, as he made a vow to The Goddess. That Excalibur would not be used in any act of aggression or murder, but would serve her with honour in the outer world. If death were to come from its blade it would be a death caused in self-defence, or defence of another. He made another vow too, as once again, he felt *Her* presence. He vowed to honour and serve her as a priest of the Old Religion. Beth would school him in its ways. And together they would bring Addie to the love of the one they called, The Goddess.

He stood, picked up the sword, and turned towards the path that wound itself down to the Sacred Well. As he did so, a warm breeze seemed to whisper, *Pendragon*. And he knew his silent vow and prayer were heard and acknowledged.

And he knew he would have need of it still.

CHAPTER TWENTY THREE: NIMUE'S ENCHANTMENT

Outside the hut, Beth could see immediately that she and Adain were alone on the Island of Godney.

She looked back inside to reassure herself that Addie still slept. The waters were shrouded in the usual mist that owed nothing to the time of day. She approached the tiny shore and strained to see through the veil. She could see nothing.

She tentatively moved closer to the lapping water, intent on dipping her feet in to check the depth, although she knew, without hesitation, that it would be too deep to wade across to Avalon. Her instincts were way off, however, when it came to Nimue. She had done her job well, and had erected a barrier of dark magic, like a dome, over Godney.

As Beth made contact with it, a bolt of energy surged through her, knocking her backwards. She staggered back, and couldn't prevent the scream of pain as it jolted its electrical charge throughout her body.

A sound, and a mother's instinct, made her turn around to see Adain standing behind her, with fear filling her eyes and etching her little face. Beth struggled to her feet, and in doing so, she pitched forwards and took another blast from Nimue's fortress wall.

The second charge bore the unmistakable blue of electricity, and the air fizzed around it. As Beth fell to her knees, Adain gave a cry of anguish and lifted her tiny hand towards the invisible dome. Her fear, anger and anguish united inside her, and shot out of her outstretched hand.

"Addie! No!"

Her cry of warning was too late and unheeded, as Beth

could feel the power of magic pour forth from her daughter, who looked up into her face with a puzzled look of uncertainty. And terror. Her actions had been instinctive, untutored, immature and uncontrolled. Beth struggled for breath as she lurched towards her.

As she reached Adain, the child dissolved into a flood of tears that could only be staunched by one person - her mother.

Beth held her close and crooned softly into her ear, nuzzling her, and rocking her gently, soothing her and protecting her from something that she knew was beyond her protection.

Nimue had left at dawn, stepping through the veil between the worlds into Glastonbury. She had searched through the veil all of the previous night, looking for the source of dark energy that she sensed was searching back. Searching for an entrance to Avalon.

She found him wandering around the veil inside Chalice Well Gardens in Glastonbury - the Sacred Well through the mirror. It was difficult whilst in the Otherworld to read his thoughts, but images of Mike and Ben came into her mind. The man was looking for them, and from the dark cloud around him she read his desperation. Someone he knew as 'The Prefect' was going to be angry with him. She sensed his fear and frustration. All of which would make him a perfect target to aid her.

She had already decided that the usurper Pendragon would not leave Avalon alive.

The man stood at the wellhead, deep in contemplation and, she suspected, prayer. He didn't look up as she moved beside him.

Eventually, he felt her presence and turned to face her.

His eyes widened at her beauty, and he felt the chains of celibacy fall from him. She smiled at him and raised her hand, her fingers curled around something he could not see. She lowered her head towards it, and blew gently. A fine red dust appeared above her hand, and as she blew on

150

it again, it settled on him in a soft caress.

Nimue had been asleep too long, now she was back in control, and now she wanted some pleasure. The man was particularly unattractive, but what mattered to her was the enchantment she would place him under. He wore the white collar of the Catholic clergy, and that gave her an additional frisson of perverse delight.

He stood enchanted before her and she leaned against him to whisper her incantation into his ear. And he was hers. Until she had finished with him.

The gardens were deserted with public opening times over. She could only guess how the man had gained entry. It wasn't difficult. She took his hand and led him from the wellhead, towards the meadow beyond, where she lay with him, taking everything, giving nothing.

Dusk was falling as she stood and pulled him to his feet, and he followed her, still deep in her spell. He would follow her anywhere, and thoughts of the Prefect and vows he had made, vanished into the void, as he was aware of nothing except her. Nimue.

She drew aside the veil again, and they stood at the water's edge of Avalon.

The man's mind was open to her and she saw in him the instrument of her revenge on Morgana, on Merlin, on Avalon. The man carried a weapon of the outer world, which she had enchanted whilst he had lain in her arms, oblivious to all but the seduction. Her spell drove him forwards as she returned to the shore and summoned the barge to return her to Godney.

He followed the path through the orchards, towards the rising smoke from the chimneys of the dwellings. Towards his target.

The first house that he came to was empty, although a fire burned brightly in the hearth and the aroma of something stewing wafted into his nostrils.

He needed to get rid of his suit and clerical collar, if he was seen attired like that, he would have no chance to carry out his task. Inside a small room to one side, he found a pile of freshly laundered clothing, from which he took a tunic and breeches and the long white robe of the druids. He balled his clothing, and tossed it into a corner, retrieving only the gun that would complete his mission, which he held between the folds of the robe.

Outside, people were moving towards the field that led to the foot of the Tor. There was an expectant air to their low chatter as he followed them, keeping his distance.

From the outside of the small crowd he could see Benjamin Lovecraft, deep in conversation with another man. To their right stood a white haired woman, supported on the arm of a younger woman. Morgana.

He felt his anger rise at what he saw as an abomination and his finger closed around the trigger, but knew he must wait. He would only get one opportunity to find them all together and he needed the sorcerer, Merlin, and the one who bore the sword to be present, too.

He would only have moments to wait, as Mike stepped back through the marker stones at the foot of the Tor where Merlin awaited him.

There were five bullets in the chamber of the man's gun. One for Morgana, one for Merlin, one each for Mike and Ben, and one for himself.

He took the safety catch off and fitted the gun with its silencer.

CHAPTER TWENTY FOUR: IN THE ARMS OF THE GODDESS

Merlin stood as Mike approached. He could see from his dirty and blood-stained condition that his journey had not been an easy one, but the sight of Excalibur in his hand brought a sigh of relief. He raised his eyebrows in question.

In reply, Mike proffered his branded forearms.

Merlin's expression became serious, as he spoke just one word. "Pendragon."

Mike had no time now for ceremony. "Take me to Godney. You say that time is different here. I'm going to get Beth and Adain and hopefully still have time in the outer world to go and get Jack."

Merlin searched his eyes and could see no remit in Mike's determination. "Very well, but you should rest first."

"I'll rest when they are all safe. Now, do you take me to Godney, or do I go alone?"

Merlin replied in a measured tone. "You should know that Morgana has seen an enchantment over the island. Nimue is no longer there, but she has placed a barrier of dark magic around Godney which even Morgana has not been able to breach. I will come with you, of course. Nimue's magic is powerful but I may be able to counter it if I am there."

They turned to return to the dwellings and Mike saw the group of people waiting at the edge of the field.

"What's that about?"

Merlin gave a smile as rare as Unicorns. "Word has spread that there is a new Pendragon. I expect they are curious."

Mike saw Morgana's white hair, and from there he easily identified Ben and Jim. He became immediately self-conscious. "Is there another way out of here?"

"You are the Pendragon now; the people of Avalon will want to greet you. Do what is right." As if to emphasise his words, Merlin gave Mike a gentle push towards them.

Father Paolo Gambini moved closer towards Morgana. Everyone's attention was on Merlin and Mike as they came down from the foot of the Tor and this would make his task all the easier, as no-one would be prepared for the carnage that would follow.

Whispers were going around the crowd, 'He carries, Excalibur. The Pendragon has returned!'

As they came closer, Merlin felt uneasy. Something was wrong. Very wrong. There was a presence in the crowd that he had felt before, a presence that was bathed in malice. He scanned the faces with concern and slowed his pace. Mike picked up on his anxiety and followed his lead, slowing his pace to match.

Paolo Gambini knew he would have to be quick. There would be no time for hesitation. The shots would have to be fired in quick succession if he was to take the advantage and complete the task that his lover had laid on him. He smiled at the memory of her, and felt once more the power of her spell.

"What is it, Merlin?" Mike whispered.

"There is one among the crowd who would do you harm. I sensed him at the mound. I sense something else too. Nimue."

"I'm ready for her."

"Don't be ridiculous. You are no match for her. Nimue is my problem. She always has been."

A face in the crowd came suddenly into focus and Merlin made ready to protect Mike. He had no idea that he and Morgana were also to die.

In the split second that followed, the man raised his

154

gun, made his choice and levelled it towards Morgana. Merlin gave a shout of warning. Estreya, ever on the alert, threw herself in front her beloved grandmother, the Lady of Avalon, as the silenced bullet found a home in her chest.

Pandemonium broke out as the man raised his gun again, this time pointing it directly at Mike.

The discharge of magic from Merlin's outstretched hand could not stop the bullet - that was the stuff of the movies - but it hit it head on and diverted its path by a fraction. It was enough to change its course so that it nicked Mike's shoulder.

Morgana was on her knees, bending over her fallen Estreya, weeping loudly and throwing all of her magic over her, but all of the magic of Avalon combined would not stay her granddaughter's approaching death. The scarlet stain on the front of her simple dress was spreading rapidly, and as she coughed, bright red bubbles appeared at the corner of her mouth. She was going to her Goddess.

Merlin's warning had caused Ben to react instantly and he launched himself at Father Paolo Gambini, recognising him from the previous night in the crypt of the ruined church. His speed belied his bulk, and he was on top of the assassin in a heartbeat. No-one would be able to say afterwards who had held the gun that blasted a hole in the man's chest - no-one cared. They would be too busy mourning one of their own.

Morgana was bereft. Her beloved granddaughter, the one who took so much joy in caring for her, was gone. She sent everyone from her house, wanting to be alone with her grief, to centre herself and be able to lead the mourners in the ceremony that would escort Estreya into the arms of the Goddess.

She sat in her chair by the dying fire, searching the embers for solace and finding none. She had been foolish to believe that she could allow one from the outer world to take the challenges of the Pendragon. She blamed herself for relaxing the rules of Avalon, no matter how much compassion she had for him. She cursed Merlin for bringing him there. She cursed herself for being weak.

Her solace came then, in the voice of the Goddess who spoke to her in her heart. Compassion was not weakness. And there were other considerations. If Adain was to become the next Lady of Avalon and unite the two worlds, then change was inevitable. Mike had conquered the challenges in the spirit of Avalon, had been accepted as the Pendragon by Erishkigal, there was to be no going back. Only forwards, cherishing the memory of her beloved Estreya and honouring her, as she rested now with the Great Mother. She would do her utmost to ensure the safety of Beth and Adain, and she would respect Mike as the Pendragon. Nimue, she would leave to Merlin of Britain.

Ayleth had slipped into Morgana's house unnoticed. She had learned the art of making no sound and leaving no trace of her presence from Estreya. Her heart was leaden in her grief for her mentor who had taught her so much, but her tears would keep until she had ensured Morgana's safety and comfort. Unbidden, she had assumed the mantle of Estreya.

Silently, she glided to Morgana's side and waited. Waited for the Lady of Avalon to return from her place of sorrow. Whatever she could do for her Lady, now and in the future, she would do. Just as Estreya had done, in laying down her life for her.

Merlin appeared at the doorway and Ayleth went to his side, hushing him, and begging him to leave in urgent whispers. Morgana raised her head and wiped the last of the tears from her ageing cheek.

"It is well, Ayleth. Come in, Merlin, old friend. Give me good news of the Pendragon."

Merlin stood before her, his face grave. Avalon had seen death and tragedy that day. He sat opposite her at her unspoken invitation. "A flesh wound. Rowan is recovered, and she has cleaned the wound and stitched it up. He will be on his feet soon enough. Morgana, I am so very sorry for the trouble that I have brought you. I should have left them in Glastonbury and be done with it. I have brought tragedy to your house this day."

Morgana struggled to find a smile. She felt sorry for him, having just been down that same road only moments before. The road of self-blame was a harsh one, and one she had no wish for him to travel. She put out her wrinkled hand and touched his face; there was too much history between them to allow his pain.

"Hush, Merlin. What is done cannot be undone and we must be grateful for the Pendragon's safety, thanks to you. Who was he?"

Merlin knew that she referred to the Prefect's man, "The Inquisition."

"Then he will soon be learning the error of his ways. It is well done. Is Benjamin all right?"

Merlin nodded. "He won't leave Mike's side, which is just as well because none of the priestesses in the infirmary are strong enough to keep him in bed. We'll make him rest for a while, he's lost some blood but there is no major damage."

Morgana nodded her satisfaction. Today was the time for putting things right. Tomorrow would be the time for grief and the ceremonies of death.

She turned to the silent girl at her side and took her hand, "Ayleth, my dear one, Merlin and I would love some tea, perhaps you would build up the fire for me?"

Ayleth's delight was immediately obvious at Morgana's acceptance of her, and her instinctive understanding, that taking on Estreya's duties was the young girl's way of honouring them both, Morgana and Estreya.

CHAPTER TWENTY FIVE: SHAPE-SHIFTING

Ayleth busied herself with the fire while Merlin and Morgana sat quietly. She turned, ready to rebuff any visitor, as she heard approaching footsteps.

Mike knocked and entered, pale and exhausted, but decidedly cleaner. He had reclaimed his own clothing and looked more himself. He went straight to Morgana.

"Lady, I am so sorry to have brought all this trouble to Avalon. I promise I will do everything in my power to put things right." He paused, "Some things can never be made right, and I will regret that forever."

Morgana stood and embraced him. "None of this is your fault, Michael. Destiny has served us a bitter blow but Avalon will always stand for what is right. Estreya would have had it no other way. We all mourn her, but neither you nor Merlin intended any harm in coming here. All I ask of you is that you seek justice for her."

Mike nodded, his expression grim. "That is certainly my intention, Lady." He turned to Merlin, "Speaking of which I've had an idea."

Merlin tilted his head on one side, ready to listen.

"Is it true that you shape-shifted Uther Pendragon into the appearance of Gorlois of Cornwall?"

Merlin sighed. "Yes, but that was long ago, and I vowed after that, that I would never do so again."

"Why?" demanded Mike.

"Because it was not well done." His mind travelled back to Cornwall, to Ygraine, Arthur's mother, and to Uther Pendragon, High King of England.

Uther had fallen in love with Ygraine, who was married to Gorlois, Duke of Cornwall. Ygraine would never agree to deceive her husband, and refused Uther at every turn. Then, there came a time when Gorlois gathered his army and stood against Uther. On the night before their last battle, Uther went to Merlin and begged him to put an enchantment on him, giving him the appearance of Gorlois, so that he could trick Ygraine into bedding him.

Merlin had his own agenda. Uther needed a son to take on the crown when he died, and Merlin needed a child who would cease the persecution of the followers of the Old Religion and practitioners of magic, so he agreed to aid in the deception. Gorlois perished that night in the battle, leaving Ygraine free to marry Uther.

Only Merlin knew that the child growing in her womb had been fathered by Uther on his night of deception. It had mattered not to Merlin, who was pleased with the outcome of his enchantment, a deception that he would later come to regret. But it was so long ago, he wondered if his magic was still powerful enough to accomplish what Mike was suggesting.

He searched Mike's eyes for a hint of his idea, but they gave him no answer. He said, "Tell me your plan."

"Ben takes Excalibur and you to the Prefect of the Inquisition. I will be there, but in the guise of his man, who now lies dead. His clothes have been found in the home of the druid whose robe he stole. Give me his appearance and I'll take his place and be in a position to be able to take them by surprise. If I walk in there with his gun to Ben's head, and tell him that unfortunately Mike Travis had tried to fight back and had died, they will accept that. He underestimates you Merlin, otherwise he would not be so easy in demanding your presence. There can only be one reason - he means to kill you. I mean to protect you. And I can do it better if he thinks I'm one of his men."

Merlin ran the plan through his mind and appeared doubtful. "I have no idea how long the enchantment will last."

"But it's worth the risk?"

Merlin appeared to make the decision. "If you are willing to risk it, then so am I."

Mike appeared satisfied. "After I bring Beth and Adain back from Godney."

Morgana interceded then. "Michael, I have seen them on Godney. They are prisoners, but they are well and cared for. It is your friend that is in the greatest danger. And if the Inquisition finds their way here, then everything that is good and wholesome in Avalon will be gone. And Avalon with it. You have sworn an oath to The Goddess that you will protect us as the Pendragon. I know how hard this is for you, but you must go back to the outer world first, and then return with Excalibur, when we will reclaim your wife and child from Nimue."

Ben's voice from the doorway claimed their attention. "She's right, Mike. The sooner we deal with this, the sooner we come back for Beth and Adain. You know what Beth would tell you to do."

He did know it, and it didn't make him feel any better. "Then let's not waste any more time", he said in a voice of stone. "Merlin?"

"And what of Nimue?"

Morgana's voice was strong and steady, "Leave Nimue to me. She is here in Avalon, I can feel her presence. I will find her and bring her here, and I will keep her occupied until you return. Go with the blessing of Avalon, Pendragon."

There was no more to be said, so the three men left Morgana at her fireside with Ayleth tending her.

Mike had donned the man's suit and clerical collar, all of which were small for Mike, the sleeves of the jacket too short and the shirt sleeves too tight. Merlin scowled at the sight of him.

They headed for Avalon's shore.

Jim was waiting for them at the landing stage. He grinned at Mike's appearance. "Suits you."

It was Mike's turn to scowl. "Funny."

Jim touched Mike on the arm and said, "Seriously, good luck, and The Goddess go with you. Come back safe and soon. I need you here for my wedding. Always after a funeral there is a celebration of joy and life. A wedding is the perfect solution. There is no reason to delay it any longer."

Mike grinned at him, "Rowan?"

"Yes. I can't believe she'll marry an old fool like me. I never thought I would have a second chance at life, let alone love. But I have. And if Estreya's passing has taught me one thing, it is that life is for taking by the scruff and living it."

"I'm glad for you, Jim. God knows there has been enough sadness and death here. A wedding will be good for everyone."

Jim laughed, "Actually, it's called a handfasting here. But by any name, a wedding there is going to be. And I want you here, standing next to me."

"Try and keep me away."

Merlin was quietly chanting the words that would part the mists and bring the barge to the shore as Jim took his leave of them.

The steady sound of oars through the lapping water broke the silence, and only moments later, the barge appeared. This time, the oars were pulled by a brown skinned man of the Faerie folk from the marshes surrounding Avalon.

He acknowledged Merlin with a short bow of his head, and sat in silence as they stepped into the barge. He pulled on the oars and the mists settled around them, silently cloaking them as they drew away from Avalon, bound for Brighid's Mound, where they would step back once again under the night sky of the outer world of Glastonbury.

None of them spoke until the barge was once more out of sight and the mists draped their damp cloak over them. Merlin's mood had darkened and he was less than happy to settle himself into the back of Mike's car, clutching Excalibur and muttering about iron beasts that belched poison into the air. He closed his eyes as Mike pulled the car out of the lane and back onto the road out of town. He kept them that way for most of the journey.

Mike's thoughts were fractured, half on Godney, half on the ruined church on the hill above Tintern. Ben knew better than to try and engage him, so for most of the way they were silent.

Dawn was breaking over the Severn as they approached the bridge that would take them back into Wales. Mike hoped that Morgana's explanation of the nature of time in Avalon meant that it was the dawn of the morning following their departure.

Merlin had opened his eyes as he sensed his own homecoming. He was crossing into the land of his birth, the land of the Cymru. His mood lightened and despite the early morning traffic, he seemed content to watch the welcoming hills.

As they reached the bridge over the Severn, he was amazed that a toll was expected. Gratified that strangers would have to pay to enter the land of his fathers, he was outraged that Welshmen were expected to do the same. He was even more outraged when Mike informed him that the toll bridge was in fact owned by the French!

It was still early when Mike drove into the car park next to the Abbey, for which he was grateful. Merlin dressed in his robe might go unnoticed in Glastonbury, but here he would stick out like a sore thumb and as Mike now carried Excalibur, he was doubly grateful. And they would be undisturbed while Merlin carried out the Charm of Becoming that would allow him to shape-shift.

Merlin was pacing at the side of the car, muttering words they couldn't hear. He stopped pacing suddenly, and turned to Mike, his eyes alight with fire.

"Get a picture of him in your head and keep it there." His voice carried authority and power.

Mike closed his eyes and pictured Father Gambini clearly. He concentrated everything he had on maintaining the image in his head.

Merlin was visualising the man too, and both of them had his image fixed in the minds. Mike almost lost the image as he looked into Merlin's eyes. There was a light emanating from behind them, reflecting the supernatural element of their undertaking.

"We will begin," Merlin said.

Mike and Ben could feel the energy intensifying and both surrendered to it.

Merlin's voice rang out, loud and clear. He began chanting The Charm of Becoming in his native Welsh tongue.

"Pwerau Ddaer, Aer, Dwr a Than
Plygwch eich pwer i fy awydd
Pwerau Tan, Dwr, Awyr a Daear
Dewch a'r newid siap nawr enedigaeth
Newid delwedd a delwedd crynu
Mae ymddangosiad newydd belach y darparu!"

Ben mentally translated the charm as Merlin chanted it.

Powers of Earth, Air, Water and Fire
Bend your power to my desire
Powers of Fire, Water, Air and Earth
Bring the shape-shift now to birth
Image change and image shiver
A new appearance now deliver!

Merlin threw out his hand and cast the final part of the spell in the language of magic.

"Arteth thaneth etheram!"

For a moment it seemed as though nothing was

164

happening, and then Mike gasped as a deep and penetrating shiver ran through him. Ben was staring at him. Mike's face seemed blurred, as if he was looking at his friend through a strong lens.

The impression cleared and Ben saw, standing next to him, Father Paolo Gambini.

"Mike? You OK?"

Mike laughed, glad that he didn't have a mirror, because inside he felt as though nothing had changed. All of his senses were still his own, and without the strange tingling all over his skin, he wouldn't have known that anything had happened to him. Outwardly he bore the appearance of Paolo Gambini, complete with white hair, flabby, pouchy skin with the texture of soft putty, framing lifeless eyes and a cruel mouth.

"Yeah, I'm fine."

Ben tried to make light of it, despite his horror at what had happened to his friend. "I've got to say, Mike, that this is not a good look for you."

Merlin stepped forwards, "Enough of the chatter, we need to move. I have no idea how long the enchantment will last."

"It lasted on Uther all night," replied Mike.

"Yes, well, that was then and this is now. We need to move."

CHAPTER TWENTY SIX: BACK IN THE CRYPT

The grass was wet and the ground spongy from rain in the night, so their footsteps were muted. The ruined church came into sight and Merlin stopped suddenly, putting a restraining hand on Mike's arm.

"If we are to have the first advantage, perhaps it would be better if you kept me as a bargaining tool."

Ben frowned. "What do you mean? You are part of the deal. No use chickening out now."

Merlin looked puzzled, "What has this to do with domestic fowl?"

Ben's anger was apparent, and Mike stepped in before the situation blew up. "What do you mean, Merlin?"

"I mean, of course I will come with you, but perhaps not in my present form? You may say you have me somewhere close by. Show them Excalibur, and tell them they can have me once your friend is released."

Mike threw the idea around in his head. "It may work. But it may screw things up."

"Just exactly what shape do you propose?" Ben demanded.

Merlin almost smiled. "You have seen it."

Mike began to be enthused by the idea. "The falcon? It may work. What about my absence?"

"Oh, that's easy. We stick to the plan. You killed Mike Travis when he tried to take Excalibur and run," replied Merlin.

Ben shifted his bulk uneasily. "I don't know, Mike. It's risky. If it goes wrong ..." His unfinished words hung in the air like a death sentence that they could be.

Mike made a decision, "It's worth the risk, this way

we'll have an unexpected advantage."

"I don't agree," Ben argued, "It's Jack's life we're gambling with. I say, we do exactly as they ask."

"Ben, there is no way that I'm going to allow them Excalibur. You must know that. I made a promise to Avalon and I'm going to keep it. If I'm going to be able to do that, we need an advantage. I have Gambini's gun, which I'm going to have stuck into the back of your neck. You will carry the sword. That is all he will see. Then I'll say I killed Mike Travis for the reason Merlin said. Then, I'm afraid it will be pretty much taking whatever chance we have."

"To do what?" Ben persisted. "You do know that we're not coming out of there without someone dying."

Mike ground his teeth. "Yeah, well, it's not going to be Jack."

Merlin spoke the Charm of Becoming again, ending with '**_Arteth thaneth etheram!_**'

Merlin's image blurred in the same way that Mike's had, eventually settling in a flurry of feathers and the cry of a bird of prey.

Mike grinned. "Holy crap, I wish I could do that."

The falcon cocked its head on one side, blinked its shiny black eyes, and gave a predatory cry. Both Mike and Ben understood the cry. '_Time to move._'

Ben took Excalibur from Mike, holding it for the first time. It seemed as though Mike was reluctant to let it go and, once in his hands, Ben understood why. The sensation of power that emanated from the sword rushed through him like a jolt of electricity. The sudden realisation of just what he was holding washed over him, and there was a new respect in his eyes. And a determination that it would not fall into the hands of the Inquisition.

They walked towards the ruined church in silence, Mike pushing Ben forwards aggressively with Gambini's gun in case there was a welcoming committee watching them. Merlin swooped ahead of them.

Inside the ruins, the trap door to the crypt was wide open and they could see the steps ahead of them in the light that came from below. A figure stepped out of the shadows. Mike drew in a long, steadying breath. What happened next would decide Jack's fate.

Monsignor Orletti pushed his large round spectacles up his nose and squinted through them. His surprise was obvious. "Father Gambini! The Prefect will be pleased." He scuttled down the steps to the crypt, an advance warning of who was behind him. Merlin glided silently on the night air, settling unheeded on a pile of rubble.

When Mike pushed Ben forwards towards the Prefect, Lucca Alessio, he did so with the barrel of the gun. Alessio stepped forwards.

"Father Gambini. I thought my instructions were to follow them. There was a problem?"

Mike swallowed and his saliva stuck in his throat. He daren't even glance towards Jack. He gave a quick bow of his head. "Your Eminence. They retrieved the sword and tried to run with it. I'm afraid I had to shoot the other one."

The Prefect narrowed his eyes, his lips in a tight line. "And the sorcerer?"

Mike grimaced. "I'm afraid they failed to bring the sorcerer forth from his tomb. He remains dead. But the sword is here."

He prodded Ben in the back with the gun. Ben's face was thunder as he held out Excalibur. His eyes hadn't left the wooden instrument of torture that held Jack, fastened by the wrists and ankles and beaten about the face, looking as if he was unconscious. He was relieved to see his chest rising and falling; at least he was alive.

The Prefect stood at the head of the Rack, ready to move his hand to the huge wheel, one turn of which could sever Jack's spine. He nodded towards Ben. "Bring it here."

Monsignor Orletti stood beside him, blinking behind

the huge round spectacles perched on his beaky nose, looking for all the world like a nervous owl. He was clearly uncomfortable with the whole proceeding. Another priest stepped from the shadows, also brandishing a gun.

Ben didn't move.

Mike gave him a huge shove with the barrel of Gambini's gun and Ben almost fell forwards.

What happened next took only seconds but seemed to play out like hours.

As Mike shoved Ben forwards, the sleeves of Gambini's suit, already too short for Mike, rode up his arms. The Pendragon brands stood out like beacons. None of them had thought to check that they had disappeared in the Charm of Becoming.

The Prefect cursed loudly, and his hand flew out towards the wheel. Two shots rang out, accompanied by a scream of agony.

The bullet from Mike's gun had hit its target - Alessio's hand. The Prefect was slumped against the rack, cradling the bloodied remains of his hand, screaming, "Kill them!" at the other priest. He turned in his agony to place his other hand on the wheel, when a falcon flew at him, talons bared, beak open, wings flapping as it screeched a deadly warning. Then it launched its fury on the Prefect.

The other priest shot at Ben and the bullet hit the blade of Excalibur in a flash of light, and fell harmlessly to the floor at Ben's feet.

Mike launched himself towards the Prefect who was trying to defend himself against the lethal talons and praying for aid that wasn't going to come to him.

Monsignor Orletti was squealing and scuttling for the steps.

Jack was moaning as the pandemonium brought consciousness back to him.

Another shot towards Mike sent his gun flying through the air, as the other priest advanced towards him, gun in his outstretched hand. Mike made an instinctive grab at the sword still in Ben's hand. He grasped it and spun around, lunging towards his assailant whose finger was already tensing around the trigger.

Mike would never be able to tell where the light came from, although at the time it seemed to have the sword as its source. It flared as he grabbed the hilt of Excalibur and he swung it in a downward arc toward the gunman. It sliced through him like a hot knife through butter, and he made no sound as he fell to the floor.

The Prefect's good arm was flailing at the bird of prey that continued to tear his flesh, his face bloodied, his mouth continuing to pray.

Orletti was long gone.

Mike took a step towards Jack and saw Alessio reach out blindly towards the wheel. If he was going down, he was going to take Jack with him.

Excalibur left Mike's hand like a javelin and, with a thud and a squelching noise, it pinned the Prefect to the wall. He slumped over it as the life left him.

Mike felt the bile rise in his throat at the carnage, but he over-rode its urgency and strode towards Jack who was staring at him through swollen and bruised eyes. He turned away and closed his eyes as Mike bent over him to release him from the leather straps.

Mike grinned as he realised that Jack was only 'seeing' Gambini. Ben hurried to the other side of the rack and began unfastening the straps. The falcon settled at the foot of the rack making a coughing sound. It was all too much for Jack and he passed out.

There was no way that they were going to get Jack on his feet. He had been fastened to the rack for over a day and he'd been beaten badly. He was disorientated as he began to come around, and was mumbling incoherently.

Ben lifted him as if he was no more than a sack of flour and hauled him up the steps into the air.

Mike and Ben were bending over him as he opened his eyes again, the cool breeze bringing returning consciousness.

"Jack! Jack, can you hear me?"

The voice was Mike's but it didn't go with the face. Jack's head ached and he abandoned the effort of trying to make sense of it.

Ben had Jack's head on his knees as he knelt on the wet grass. "Jack?"

Jack tried to focus, but images were drifting in and out, impressions coming and going, when his attention was drawn to a tall, middle-aged man in what looked like a druid's robe, coughing feathers from his mouth.

Jack looked at Mike, his eyes wide. "Did he just eat that bird?" And then he passed out again.

When consciousness returned once more, his eyes were clear beneath the swelling. Mike had taken off the jacket of Gambini's suit and put it around Jack. He had ripped off the white collar and cast it away. The sleeves of the shirt, too tight, had been opened and rolled up. Jack tried to sit up, but Ben shook his head and gently pressed him down onto the ground again.

Merlin stood before Mike, ready to chant the Charm of Undoing. He raised his hands on high and his voice rang out.

> "*Pwerau Ddaer, Aer, Dwr a Than*
> *Plygwch eich pwer i fy awydd*
> *Pwerau Tan, Dwr, Awyr a Daear*
> *Gwrthdroi'r siâp-sifft roi genedigaeth*
> *Newid delwedd a delwedd crynu*
> *Mae'r hen ymddangosiad bellach yn darparu!*
> *Arteth thaneth etheram!*

> Powers of earth, Air, Water and Fire
> Bend your power to my desire
> Powers of Fire, water, Air and earth
> Reverse the shape-shift given birth
> Image change and image shiver

The old appearance now deliver!

It looked to Jack as if 'Gambini' was shimmering, then everything blurred. The shimmering returned and then Mike was standing next to him.

"Mike! Neat trick."

Mike leaned over him. "You okay?"

Jack's expression was grim with his mouth set in a serious line. Pain was written in his eyes as he said quietly, "I feel a bit ... taller. Nice tats by the way." He tried to grin at Mike but failed, as he pointed to the Pendragon branding on his arms.

Before Mike could gather an answer, Jack was out again.

CHAPTER TWENTY SEVEN: NIMUE AND MORGANA

Morgana had sent out a party of Druids to search for Nimue, or signs of her at least. Her vision had told her that she was still not on the Isle of Godney, and that Beth and Adain were safe. Her senses told her that Nimue was in Avalon. Her instructions to the men were to find her and 'invite' her to Morgana's house.

Before Nimue had broken with Avalon, she and Morgana had been friends, great friends. Morgana had grieved for her as she witnessed her decline, Nimue unable to handle the awesome power of Merlin's magick. But the inherent problem with magic was knowing when and when not to use it. It wasn't to be used lightly, and Nimue had fallen under its own spell. She had begun to live for the power until it took over her mind, her whole being, her soul. She had become power hungry for the sake of power itself, and it had twisted her, corrupted her, as surely as any deathly disease. Morgana felt that Nimue was as much a victim of the power as those that she wielded it against.

Her heart was heavy but she knew what she must do.

While she awaited Nimue, she reached out once more to Godney. She didn't have the power to bring down Nimue's barrier - that would take hers and Merlin's power combined. Her power was fading with the advancing centuries, whereas Nimue's was still fresh after her long sleep. She could see through the barrier though, and now she would try and communicate through it.

She closed her eyes and slowed her breathing and her heart rate, bringing on her trance with accomplished ease.

She searched the mists surrounding Avalon, until she came to the small island in the water that was Godney, where Beth and the child were seated on the grass outside the hut. Beth was cradling Adain, and Morgana smiled as she realised that Beth was singing to the child.

She reached out to Beth first. "Beth, can you hear me?"

There was no reaction from her; she was totally focussed on finding a way off the island. Nothing else would penetrate her thoughts. And then, just as Morgana had decided to try and connect with Adain, she heard the child's voice. She smiled. She had not been wrong about the child; she was in truth, in all ways, her successor.

The small voice found its home in her consciousness. *'Lady Morgana, please help us. Mother is afraid and my infant voice has no words of comfort. Please send help.'*

When the soul speaks, it finds its own language.

"All is well, child. You are safe and someone will come for you soon. Remain calm. That is the best way to help your mother at this moment."

Unwilling to distress Adain, Morgana soothed her further and then cut the connection gently. She opened her eyes to a darkened fire and bent to feed it with another log.

It wasn't a physical blow from behind, but the effect was the same as she went sprawling onto the floor in front of the dying fire.

Nimue stood behind her, her hand outstretched towards Morgana, her dark magic having found its target.

Morgana gasped as she tried to stand.

"Nimue ... "

"How dare you stand against me, old woman? How dare you challenge my power? You think to deny me as the next Lady of Avalon in favour of a mewling child? Well, I have that child and although I will refrain from taking your life, I will return as Lady of the Lake and once again be the guardian of Excalibur. For I demand its return. How dare you believe that one from the outer world is worthy to carry the sword of Pendragon? Avalon has gone soft! It is no longer a power in the land, but I will return it to that power, and then we will see who shall be Lady of Avalon.

And when your time is done, as it will be soon, I shall take your place, and neither you, nor Merlin, will stop me. Take this warning as a token of our previous friendship, for it is the last you will receive!"

"Nimue, please, listen to me. Avalon still has its power, but it remains untainted, uncorrupted. The time will come when once again it will be accessed by the outer world, its power to heal acknowledged. But that will never be while the power is dark. Return to the light Nimue, and save yourself."

"Do not deign to patronise me, Morgana. You may not live to regret it." Her hand shot forth again, spewing forth her malice in the shape of magic, and Morgana fell senseless onto the hearth rug.

On Godney, Adain sensed the hurt to Morgana, and the part of her soul that was aware of it found voice. Adain began to scream.

Beth could not even get close to her as she flailed her arms wildly; thrashing the air and screaming like a banshee. Beth was consumed with fear for her daughter and looked about frantically for the source of her distress. She could find none.

Suddenly, Adain's eyes filled with a strange light behind their usual sapphire, her face became set, and she cast her hand outwards towards Nimue's barrier. The energy hit the barrier with full force and exploded in a flash of light that rebounded back as if from a mirror, hitting Beth square on the chest, and rendering her unconscious before she had time to scream.

Adain screamed for her.

Nimue heard her screams in Avalon and hurried to the shore to summon the barge from the mists. Adain was her trump card in the game they were playing and she daren't let any harm befall her. That would be game over.

On the shore of Godney, Nimue passed through her own barrier and hurried to Adain. As she approached her, she smiled at the almost lifeless body of the child's mother.

177

Good. If she died, that would save her the trouble. She stepped over Beth's inert body and went to Adain.

She grasped her small wrists and pulled her to her chest, enfolding her in arms that had never known the true meaning of love. Adain struggled to be free of her, but Nimue held her both by physical strength and by magic. Adain fell silent as the dark energy wrapped itself around her and she began to cry as she looked at Beth.

Once more, there had been no understanding, no control, over her instinctive magic. Nimue smiled, she was going to enjoy the tutoring of this child.

In Avalon, Ayleth had returned to find Morgana lying in front of the fire, and had quickly sounded the alarm, and called for the healer priestesses to attend her.

Morgana opened her eyes to the realisation of one thing. Nimue had to be dealt with once and for all time. But Avalon had seen enough death in recent days, and to kill without reason or mercy was not the way of Avalon.

But she had a plan. And it would need Mike and Merlin to see it happen.

CHAPTER TWENTY EIGHT: RETURN TO AVALON

Mike and Merlin had over-ruled Ben, who wanted to take Jack home to his cottage and take care of him. They both knew that the healing powers of Avalon would not only bring him back to health more quickly, but it would strengthen his weakened spirit. Despite Jack's attempt at his usual humour, he was depleted and desperately in need of healing.

Between them they got Jack back to Mike's car, where he drifted in and out of consciousness. In a more lucid moment he caught hold of Mike and nodded towards Merlin.

"Who *is* that guy? He's weird."

"You won't believe me if I tell you," Mike said quietly.

"Try me."

Mike grinned. "He's Merlin. Merlin of Britain."

"You mean, *the* Merlin? Merlin the magician? King Arthur's Merlin?"

"Yep."

"Really? Fucking really?"

"Yes, Jack. Now lean back and go to sleep. We've got to get going."

"Where?"

"Avalon."

Jack closed his eyes, already half way to oblivion again, and muttered something incoherent. Mike put his hand on his forehead and frowned. Jack was burning up.

The journey to Glastonbury seemed to take longer than usual, but that was due to each one of them harbouring heavy thoughts. Jack slept all the way, but his sleep wasn't peaceful. He continued to mumble and his fever was

179

rising. He needed care in a hurry.

When they reached the western gateway of Brighid's mound, Mike woke him while Merlin opened the gateway and called the barge from the mists. It took both him and Ben to get Jack safely into the barge.

At the landing stage Jim was waiting for them.

"I don't know how you knew we were coming," said Mike, "But I'm very glad to see you. Jack is in desperate need of Rowan's care. Can we take him to the infirmary straight away?"

"Of course. Follow me. As for how I knew, the answer is I didn't. I was here watching for someone else."

Mike didn't comment, but he noted the strain on Jim's face.

"Mike, let Ben and I take Jack to the infirmary. I think you should go and see Morgana. It's important."

Mike scanned Jim's face for further information, but he could see it was closed. He nodded his understanding and relinquished Jack into his and Ben's care.

Morgana appeared to be seated in the same position as he had left her, except the lines on her face looked deeper and she was clearly very tired.

"Morgana? Jim asked me to come straight here. Is something wrong? Well ... more wrong than before?"

Morgana raised her head to him and smiled. He could see the concern in her eyes.

"Is it Beth? Adain? Tell me!"

"Sit down Michael. Yes, there is news. It seems that there has been ... an accident. Beth is hurt," she raised her hand to prevent him interrupting her. "She is being cared for in the infirmary Nimue, it seems, is not totally heartless, or she deemed Beth as irrelevant - whatever the reason -Nimue summoned the barge to bring Beth here. Rowan and the healer priestesses are looking after her."

He was half way to the door, "What the hell happened?" he demanded.

Morgana hesitated, then after a heavy sigh she said, "It

appears that Adain cast out a heavy blast of uncontrolled magic and it rebounded on Beth."

"*Adain*? What are you saying?"

"I'm saying that your daughter has the gift of magic, Michael. It is unschooled, and way out of control. We need to get her to the stone circle and perform a ritual that will curb her abilities so that they can develop at a natural pace. If we do not, she will do great harm to herself and to others."

"Then let's do it!"

"Firstly, we do not have Adain. She is still with Nimue. And secondly you will not be a part of the ritual. It is a deeply spiritual ceremony performed only by the women of Avalon. In other circumstances Beth would have been there, but she will not be well enough. If she recovers in time, then she will of course, be there. We are doing everything we can to bring Adain here. I fear there is only one way to do that. And that is to give Nimue what she wants."

Mike dragged his hand through his hair, clearly he was about to explode. "Morgana, I don't care what it takes, get her back! If anything happens to her, I will hold you personally responsible. It is your *plan*, your *meddling* in our lives, that has brought this on us. You do what you have to do, to get her back! I'm going to Beth!"

He met Merlin at the door, and pushed past him in his distress.

Merlin could see Morgana's anguish immediately. "What has happened, Lady? Is there anything that I can do to assist in whatever is distressing you and the Pendragon?"

"Thank you, Merlin, my old and dear friend. I sometimes think that the hope of Avalon connecting with the outer world again is a dream that should not come into being. Our ways are too hard for them."

Merlin was quiet for a moment, and then he said, "I think you underestimate them, Morgana. They have a great resilience of spirit, a fierce loyalty to those they love, and many are returning to The Goddess. Give them time. I believe your hopes are not unfounded." He nodded towards Mike's quickly retreating steps, "That one is worthy of your trust. He is worthy of the title Pendragon. Perhaps that is enough for now. Let the future unfold gently. Now, tell me what has happened."

"Always wise council, Merlin. I will heed your word, despite the fact that you have returned with the look of a much younger man!"

She laughed at him, and then became serious again almost immediately as she explained things to him.

"While you were gone, I had a visit from Nimue. She has made it perfectly clear that she will stop at nothing to take my place and, if I am not mistaken, she doesn't want to wait until I hear the raven's call in the natural way of things. She has changed, Merlin, corrupted and twisted by the power. I am no match for her now. She has the child still, and that is another problem. Adain has the magic of Avalon, and it is out of control in one so young. She threw out some dark energy born of fear, and it has hurt Beth. She is very seriously ill, in a deep and unnatural sleep, a coma, I believe they call it in the outer world. Rowan is with her constantly, but I fear for her. It doesn't look good. I am tired, Merlin, but I will carry on as Lady of Avalon while there is breath in my body. I hope I have the strength to last until the young one is old enough to succeed me."

Merlin smiled at her, "You, Lady, are tougher than you give yourself credit for. It's been a bad day, that's all. I'll get Ayleth to make you a sleeping potion. I am here now, and you can rest. After all, the Pendragon is back."

Morgana leaned forwards and plucked a falcon's feather from his hair. "Still out of practice, I see." They laughed together, and she visibly relaxed. Merlin was right - the Pendragon was back, and he looked as though he was ready for battle.

CHAPTER TWENTY NINE: THE COUNCIL OF AVALON

Jack was responding remarkably well to the ministrations of Rowan's assistant. Ben never left his side unless he had to. Beth, on the other hand, seemed to be slipping deeper into her unnatural sleep.

"I'm taking her out of here," Mike snapped at Morgana. "She needs a hospital and modern medicine, a real doctor and not herbs and mumbo jumbo!"

Morgana rested her hand on his shoulder. "Of course, Michael, if that is what you want, but please listen to me first. Beth has been hit by a very powerful and dark magic. Your doctors cannot begin to understand what is at the root of this. While she is in this deep state, she is journeying. If her soul wishes it, she will return to us. We are doing everything that we know to counteract this magic. It is taking time because the magic was unformed and chaotic, but I believe in Rowan's ability to bring her through this. If you take her back to your world, what will you tell your doctors? The truth? How will that help her? Trust me Michael, I want to see her well again just as much as you do. You spoke the truth when you said it was my fault, and I am deeply sorry."

Mike looked at her pained eyes. "No, Morgana, it isn't. I spoke in anger and I apologise. How long do you think she will be like this? She will come back, won't she?" His voice cracked.

Morgana turned away from his tears, unwilling for him to see her own. There was a heavy ache in her heart and she knew she was no good to him in that state. She summoned Rowan to return to Beth's bedside and went in search of Merlin.

Jim was at the far end of the infirmary, joking with Jack. He looked up and saw Mike's distress and made his way over to him.

"They're doing everything they can, Mike. For both of them. Morgana is going to give Nimue whatever she wants to get Adain back. She'll not be harmed, not while Nimue needs her."

"Is there no other way?"

Jim shook his head and smiled. Mike had never seen him look so well and so happy and he was glad for him.

"Why won't they let me go there and just take her?"

"Because Morgana has seen enough death in recent days and that would be the outcome of it. Probably yours."

""I can't just wait around for something to happen. I need to *do* something."

"I know. But give it a little longer: Morgana will send for Nimue, and in the meantime, Adain is safe." He looked down at Beth's still, pale face. "Morgana and Merlin will bring her through, I'm sure of it. Why don't you go and get some rest, Mike. You look done in. Eat something at least. You need your strength."

Mike needed to change the subject. "Tell me about Rowan. She's very lovely."

"Too lovely for me, I think. I don't know what she sees in me. There are plenty of young Druids who would change places with me in an instant. I'm an old man!"

Mike laughed. "You're a good man, Jim. And you look in better shape than me. I hope you'll be happy, you deserve that."

"I feel like I have a second chance, Mike. Rowan is teaching me about the healing powers of herbs and about other forms of healing. I spend most of my time here, helping where I can, and learning. I've found something here that I never knew before, I've found my soul."

"I understand you've done a lot for Jack. Thanks for that."

Jim laughed. "He's fine, hasn't lost his sense of

humour. He cracks me up."

Mike grinned. "I'll be over to see him in a minute."

Jim nodded his understanding and left.

Mike bent over Beth and kissed her gently on her cool cheek. "Come home, Beth. We need you. I need you."

There was a commotion outside the infirmary and a couple of the priestesses went to see what was happening. One of the younger women returned and went straight over to Mike.

"Lady Morgana has asked for you. Will you come with me, please?"

Mike followed her without hesitation. Jim was outside the infirmary and people were making their way out of the village.

"What's happening, Jim?"

"Morgana has called a meeting of the Council of Avalon. And she wants you there."

This was something new to Mike. "The Council of Avalon? Is that what it sounds like?"

Jim nodded. "Yes. Twelve of the elders, made up of six druid elders and six senior priestesses, and Morgana, meet at the Sacred Well. It's usual when there is an important decision to be made."

Mike's face betrayed his fears. "This is about Addie, isn't it? What are they planning that needs Council approval?"

"I believe Morgana intends to surrender her position to Nimue, to grant her demands, in exchange for Adain."

"What? No! She can't do that, there must be another way."

Jim could give him no more, so he simply nodded towards the sacred Well. "Best you get off and hear what they have to say."

"Aren't you coming?"

Jim shook his head with a smile. "No. Council members and invited guests only. You can tell me all about it later. Go on. I told you once; it's not polite to keep a

Lady waiting."

Mike turned quickly on his heel and ran towards the Sacred Well. Two druids standing at the entrance to the well stood aside to let him pass.

At the wellhead, the members of the Council of Avalon stood in a circle around Morgana, who was seated. Merlin stood at her side.

Morgana rose from her seat and addressed them.

"I have served as Lady of Avalon for many centuries. I am old and soon Avalon will need a new Lady. There is one, a child still. She is the daughter of the Pendragon and she has the gifts. However, Nimue has her held captive on Godney. She has promised to release her on certain conditions. Her demands are simple - she will become my successor. She is a daughter of Avalon, also with the gifts, she is more than qualified. And she wants Excalibur."

She paused, watching their faces intently, then continued. "I am willing to agree to her demands, but I cannot do so without your blessing. This decision will affect Avalon forever. Please speak now."

She took her seat again.

One of the senior druids took a step forwards. He bowed his head briefly. "Lady Morgana, I am Eldred, and I speak for the Druids. I think you know that we have knowledge of this, and we are grateful that you seek our council. It is our feeling that this would be wrong for Avalon. Nimue has turned away from us and only seeks to return under these conditions to satisfy her own hunger for power. We feel that Avalon would not be in safe hands. Is there nothing else that can be done?"

He bowed again and returned to his place in the circle.

Morgana acknowledge him with a return bow of the head. "Is there any-one else who will speak?"

The oldest of the priestesses stepped forwards and bowed her head to Morgana. "I am Enndolyn, and I speak for the Priestesses. We could not show allegiance to Nimue. We feel that her dark magic will eventually destroy

Avalon and we would not see her as your successor. In our eyes it would be a blasphemy." She bowed again to Morgana. "Lady," she said as she returned to her place.

Morgana acknowledged her respect and returned it with a bow of her head.

"Anyone else?"

Mike pushed forwards between two of the Druids. He bowed his head to Morgana.

"I am the Pendragon, and I speak for my daughter and for Avalon. I have sworn an oath to protect you with Excalibur. I shall not see it returned into such hands and tainted by dark magic. And I will not see this place brought down by Nimue. It would be easy for me to say, yes, do what Nimue wants and have my daughter returned immediately. My wife lies in your infirmary, near to death, and it would be easy for me to take her from here. But I believe in Avalon. And if you once agree to this, can you trust her? I would rather put my trust in myself, and Morgana, and Merlin. I say we find another way."

Morgana stood and leaned on Merlin, already missing the support of Ayleth's arm. As one, the Council members took a step forwards. Merlin nodded his approval.

He turned to Mike. "That means that they unanimously support you. Now we'd better come up with a plan."

Morgana took a step forwards and bowed her head again and, as she turned to leave - signalling the end of the meeting - Mike saw the glistening of tears in her eyes. He clenched his teeth, bringing the scar on his cheek into prominence again.

He walked with Morgana and Merlin back to her house as the Council dispersed. "I meant what I said. You have put your faith in me, now I must honour it. I will do whatever you ask of me."

Morgana smiled, "Spoken like a true Pendragon. Faith in you we have, but I'm afraid you can never stand against her power. There was a time, long ago, when I was a match for her, but no longer."

Merlin signalled for Ayleth to come to her Lady. "Send for Nimue, Morgana. Ask her to come and claim the succession."

Morgana raised an eyebrow. "The Council were very clear ..."

"No!" shouted Mike. "No, Merlin, you can't."

"Send for her, Morgana and I promise that I will deal with it this time. Nimue has always been my problem. If I had the courage last time, none of this would be happening."

Morgana's face seemed paler. "Merlin, it is not our way. Please don't do this."

"What?" demanded Mike, "What is he talking about? Morgana?"

Morgana shivered and Ayleth immediately went for her shawl. When she had draped it around her shoulders she stepped outside.

"Merlin plans to use magic to kill her." She turned to the doorway to call Ayleth, but the girl was already returning to her side. "Ayleth, please send word to Nimue on Godney that Morgana, the Lady of Avalon, wishes to speak with her regarding her succession, and asks that she bring the child."

Ayleth left without a sound.

The silence was heavy and none of them wanted to break it.

CHAPTER THIRTY: DEADLY PLANS

Eventually it was Merlin who spoke. "I must go and prepare. Nimue must have no clue as to what I plan. Please excuse me."

Morgana seemed to have aged visibly. "There will be a price," she said softly.

Mike was still agitated. "What price?"

She explained patiently, "When magic is used to kill, the one casting the spell forfeits a part of him or herself. Merlin will have to be very quick if he is not to be the one we lose. He is taking a grave risk, and one of which I do not approve, but I see no other alternative."

"And you're all right with this?"

"It is not a matter of being all right. It's about protecting Avalon. I have no doubt that Nimue will destroy it given the opportunity. She has killed already, and when she has done here, she will look to the outer world to gain her power. Is that what you want?"

Mike couldn't get his head around the enormity of what Morgana was saying. "But killing her? Can't you just send her to some ... phantom zone, or something?"

Morgana gave a harsh laugh. "She has already returned from our version of that, as you well know. And besides all that, you are right: we couldn't trust her to return Adain. Leave me now, Pendragon. Go to your wife. Ayleth will make me some tea and I will rest."

Mike had never felt so helpless. He was supposed to be the Pendragon, the wielder of Excalibur, he should have a part in this. He went off to find Merlin.

He found him deep in thought at the Sacred Well. He turned around at Mike's approach.

"Come to talk me out of it, Pendragon?"

"I wish, just for once, you'd call me by my name. It's Mike."

Merlin scowled. "In Avalon, you now bear the name Pendragon. Get used to it."

"Merlin, is there really no other way? Killing in self-defence is one thing, but in cold blood ...?"

Merlin gave a now familiar scowl. "Haven't the stomach for it? Then I suggest you don't watch."

Mike's frustration and fear all boiled down into something akin to cabbage soup, and it boiled over. "Don't watch! In case you've missed it, my daughter and my wife are at the centre of this. It's *my* responsibility to deal with it, not yours."

"And how exactly do you intend to do that?"

"I have Excalibur now. Nimue wants it, and I want my family back. Fair exchange."

Merlin's anger exploded into ground zero. "You forget yourself, Pendragon! Excalibur is not yours to bargain with! It is in sacred trust to you and it must *never, ever,* fall into the hands of Nimue again. Understand me - Nimue is mine to deal with. You will have a part to play in the charade that will give me the opportunity to speak the Spell of Death, that's all."

"The Spell of Death?"

Merlin hesitated before replying. "Once spoken, it will find a home either in the intended target, or otherwise. It has to be precise, for once it is out, there is no stopping it. If anyone should get in the way of it, they will die."

"Can't you just put her back to sleep?"

"You are, and always will be, welcome in Avalon, Pendragon, but do not imagine that entitles you to interfere with our decisions. There will be times when Avalon will have need of you, and times when you have need of Avalon, but this is not such a time. Nimue is a killer, and a destroyer, and the Gods know I am to blame for that. I succumbed to her seduction and gave her power that she could not control. I sentenced her to death then. I must pay for it now. Believe me, if there was another way, I would take it."

Mike saw the pain in Merlin's eyes. "You still love her."

"Yes, I still love her. But I *will* kill her. And you will not interfere."

Mike could *feel* Merlin's pain then. He understood love, and what it could do. He had killed in defence of his family, and when he had returned to the crypt of the ruined church to free Jack, he knew that it would end in killing. Was this really any different? Nimue had been responsible for Adain's imprisonment and was, in some way, responsible for Beth's condition. She had used magic to manipulate Gambini into killing Estreya, and he believed she had killed and would kill without mercy to achieve her goals. Merlin was right - this wasn't his world. But maybe it was his fight.

"Tell me what I can do," he said quietly.

Merlin nodded. "You must hand over Excalibur to her. That is the only thing that will distract her long enough for me to speak the spell. Until that moment she will be on her guard and will have protection around her. At the moment she takes Excalibur from you she will be vulnerable, but only for a second. If I miss that window of opportunity, Excalibur will be lost. Avalon will be lost."

"Then I will make sure you don't miss it."

Merlin nodded again. "Pendragon, once you hand her the sword you must get out of the way, because the instant she touches it, I shall speak the Spell of Death, you understand what I'm saying?"

"Yep. Duck or have my arse blasted off."

Merlin looked puzzled. "What has a water fowl to do with this?"

Mike grinned. "No! 'Duck'- it means get out of the ... never mind."

Merlin retreated into his own head again, so Mike walked steadily back to the village. He needed to think too, and he headed for the Tor.

As he approached through the field at the foot of the Tor, he was surprised by people pushing carts containing long staves of wood. He watched as they stood them upright, connecting them with a sturdy platform. Then he understood.

It was Estreya's funeral pyre.

It wasn't Morgana's words of wisdom, nor Merlin's heartache, that set his course, nor even Adain's capture, it was the sight of this final act of love for Morgana's gentle, beautiful granddaughter, who had lived to love the Lady and Avalon, that hardened him to what was to come. Whatever he could do for her, he would do.

His spirit needed lifting, and he knew where to go to make that happen.

Jack had been released from Rowan's clutches in the infirmary, and was seated at one of the large round tables in the Meeting House, a huge plate of food in front of him and a goblet of wine in his hand. His face was a multi-coloured kaleidoscope of bruises but the swelling around his eyes had almost gone, revealing the ever–present twinkle of mischief that was better belonging to a child. Jack was back.

He clapped him on the back. "Hey Jack, you're looking ... better."

Jack grinned at him. "You should have some of this wine, Mike, it's made with apples and honey and all sorts of herbs and stuff. Let me pour you one."

"No thanks Jack. I've got to keep a clear head."

Jack's face clouded over momentarily. "I'm sorry, that was insensitive of me. I just..."

"I know. It's all right It's all going to be all right." He needed a change of subject. "Where's Ben?"

"Catching up on some kip. He hasn't slept since we got here. And from the look of you, neither have you. What can I do? You know I love Beth, and Addie is my god-daughter - you know how much I love her. Tell me, Mike, whatever you need."

"Having you back in one piece is enough for now. How are you?"

Jack grinned at him again, "I'm fine, really."

"Really?"

"Yes. Mike, about Ben and I. I need to talk to you. He's celibate. He doesn't want ... doesn't need ..."

Mike held up a hand. "I know what celibate means, Jack, you don't need to paint me a picture. And right now, that's information overload!" he paused and drew a deep breath, "I'm sorry. It's just ..."

"Yeah, I know, too bloody much, right? It's okay, Mike. I get it."

Mike let his head fall; everything seemed too heavy at that moment. After a minute or two, he looked up into Jack's eyes. "You're okay with that?"

Jack nodded slowly, a broad smile creeping across his face. "I really am. It's over-rated anyway."

Mike took his meaning and smiled back at him. "So, what now?"

"Now, we go on as before. He has his world and I have mine. They're miles apart, but sometimes they reach a neutral point. I'll settle for that."

"You shouldn't settle for anything less than what makes you happy. Life's too short, Jack."

Jack grinned, and winced at the pain it caused. "Then I'll settle for what makes me happy. I *am* happy. When we get back, I'm going to move into the cottage for a while. The business is ticking over nicely, Brody is a bloody marvel and more than ready for a partnership. Then, when I can't stand the no water, no electricity, no TV and all that, I'll bugger off to my apartment for a couple of days to reconnect with the crazy world out there. You won't get rid of me that easily. What about you?"

"Oh, you know, nothing much. I'm just about to go and help Merlin of Britain kill an evil sorceress, nothing out of the ordinary."

Jack had been in the process of sipping at his wine. He

snorted, inhaled it, coughed a lot, and then they both dissolved into laughter at the incongruity of it all.

Mission accomplished. Mike's spirit was well and truly lifted.

But it didn't take away from the truth of the matter. Nimue was about to die.

CHAPTER THIRTY ONE: THE SPELL OF DEATH

Mike sat with Beth while he waited.

After an hour, Ayleth appeared at the bedside. "My Lady Morgana has asked for your presence. She awaits you at the Sacred Well. You know the way?"

Mike nodded. Was this another meeting of the Council? Had they changed their minds?

He made his way to the well. Merlin awaited him at the entrance. He was holding Excalibur. Mike's heart sank; they were going through with it. He took Excalibur from Merlin and immediately felt its power surge through him. This was the very reason that such as Nimue could never wield it.

"Nimue is here. She is on her way from the shore as we speak. I have to tell you, she is alone. She has not brought your daughter with her. But Adain is no longer a prisoner on Godney. She is in the safe hands of the men from the marshes, she is under an enchantment and she is well and happy. Nimue's insurance I think. Come."

Morgana stood in the spot where she had previously held Council, but this time there was no chair. This time, her duty required her to stand. Stand against an enemy of Avalon.

She acknowledged Mike with a brief nod of her head and stood firm.

There was a sudden flurry of activity, and Nimue was before them. Mike had to acknowledge her beauty. She was breathtaking, despite her great age, but her beauty was the product of her powerful magic. Mike knew that her beauty was superficial; inside she was ugly, twisted, tainted. It made him feel slightly better about what he was about to take part in. Deception and death.

Morgana took a step towards her. "Avalon bids you welcome, Nimue, Lady of the Lake. The Council of Avalon has considered your request."

Nimue interrupted her before she could speak further. The malice in her voice made Mike feel queasy.

"*Request?* I have no request, Morgana. I *demand* the return of Excalibur from the Pretender who dares to call himself, Pendragon! I *demand* my right of succession! And I demand it now."

"You demand a great deal, Nimue. But I see you have brought little in return."

"You can have the brat! She is with the men of the marshes - but you already know that, your spies are everywhere. They have instructions to bring her here in one hour. If you refuse my demands I will give them other instructions. I think you understand my meaning."

Mike's grip on Excalibur tightened, and he closed his eyes to restrain himself from reacting to the obvious implication and taunt. He sensed Merlin watching him closely.

Morgana continued. "You have given me no reason to trust you, Nimue. But the Council has decided to grant your demands. You may take Excalibur, and on my death you will succeed me as Lady of Avalon. I expect that day will now be sooner than before. But it is of no matter, I am tired. You are welcome to it."

There was a brief second of uncertainty that flickered across Nimue's face. She had come for a fight, and it wasn't going to happen. It was quickly replaced by triumph. She took a step forwards and held out her hands.

"Excalibur," she said.

Mike walked towards her, his face a blank canvas, his mind on full alert. He had to be ready. He held out the sword and placed it in Nimue's hands.

A fragment of time seemed to stand still as her triumph exploded onto her face. Mike threw himself sideways,

Morgana turned away, and Merlin drew himself up to his full height, his hand thrust out towards her, his voice echoing throughout Avalon and beyond:

"Eskereth mort akenshar, Nimue!"

The flash of lightening was blinding. Nimue didn't have time to scream as she fell to the floor, a wrinkled gnarled old crone. She was beautiful no more. She was alive no more.

Mike had been holding his breath, and he exhaled in a moment of what seemed like anti-climax. That was that, then. The Spell of Death. Just a few words of mumbo jumbo and the powerful Nimue was no more. It didn't seem real. None of it seemed real. He picked up the fallen Excalibur and turned to Merlin.

And he took an involuntary step backwards at the sight of him.

Gone was the handsome man of early middle age. Merlin stood before them, bent and arthritic, his hair was past his shoulders and whiter that the whitest snow. His beard matched it in colour and length. His years were etched into his features like an inscription on a tomb. Mike remembered Morgana's words. *'When magic is used to kill, the one casting the spell forfeits a part of him or herself.'*

Well, he'd done that all right. Done it for Avalon. For Morgana. For Adain. And in many ways, for him.

Morgana was at Merlin's side - two ancient souls who had given everything. Mike approached them, and without thinking, he knelt on one knee, laid Excalibur at their feet, and picked up Morgana's hand and kissed the back of it.

"I, the Pendragon, give you my oath, that whenever you have need of me, I will be there for you. My Lady. Merlin of Britain."

Morgana touched his shoulder. "We know. And we thank you. Please get up. Look," she said, pointing past his shoulder.

Mike turned around. Beth was standing at the entrance to the well, a bewildered look on her face. Mike looked

197

equally confused.

Merlin smiled at him. "A life for a life, Pendragon. That's how it has always been. Everything in balance. Nimue's death ended her magic and the effects of it, directly or indirectly.

Before he could move, Ayleth appeared from the landing stage. She was walking slowly, holding the chubby little hand of his daughter.

Morgana said gently, "Go, Pendragon. Be with your family."

"I believe, I already am. If it is acceptable, I wish to attend the funeral of Estreya. It is to be today?"

Morgana nodded, "You will be welcome."

Adain broke the solemnity with a squeal of delight at seeing her mother, and as Beth gathered her daughter into her arms, she beamed at Mike. She knew there was a world between them, and things that he would tell her and things that he wouldn't, but they could wait. For now, she was just happy.

Morgana and Merlin watched them walk back towards the village. Morgana linked her arm through his, "Life may be for the young, Merlin, but while we have breath, I believe we are entitled to our share. What do you think?"

"I think I need a chair and your fireside, and I think ... I would like a cup of tea."

CHAPTER THIRTY TWO: TWO FUNERALS

All of Avalon had gathered at the foot of the Tor in front of Estreya's pyre.

She was laid on the platform in a beautiful gown of sage green silk and there was a garland of flowers in her hair and a posy in her hands. She was about to go through the Rite of Crossing.

It was a celebration of the earthly life of one who has passed into the Summerland, a sending off on their journey to another plane of existence. It was an acknowledgement of an ending, and a beginning.

Morgana walked through the waiting mourners, herself in mourning, but with the dignity of one of her position. She would grieve for Estreya later, in the privacy of her own home. Now she had to direct the grief of the others to a place of acceptance and expectation of meeting Estreya again.

Her robe was of white silk and she too wore a garland of flowers in her hair. She looked serene, almost bridal, as she stood in front of her granddaughter's pyre, which was flanked on either side by a druid bearing a flaming torch.

The atmosphere was heavy and hushed as Morgana began the ceremony.

"Hearken to the words of the Dark Goddess, She who has been ever present, as Maiden, Mother and Dark Mother. She who has been known to us as Morrigan, Hecate, Arianrhod and Cailleach. Hearken to her words:

'I who am the Washer at the Ford, the Keeper of the Dark Cauldron, the Lady of Changes. I am the Dark Mother who knows the number of your days, and it is I who calls out to your soul in the darkness of night. It is I

199

who will comfort you at the hour of your crossing, and it is I who will escort you to the Summerland. Do not fear me, for I am that which you are, have been, and will be. Do not fear the ever turning wheel of life, which turns from light to darkness and into light again. Remember that as night follows day and becomes morning, so your soul will rest between lifetimes. When soul lessons are learned and karma is in balance, it is I that greets you as One with the Cosmos, One with All That Is."

She closed her eyes and steadied her voice, then continued.

'Greet me with joy, not sorrow - with peace, not fear. Come to me when your earthly life is done. Come to me when you hear the raven's call, and I will spin the web of life for you. I am Arianrhod, Lady of Changes, Lady of the Silver Wheel turning; I am the Morrigan, calling to you from the Ford with the voice of my crows and ravens. I am the Dark Mother.'

Morgana paused and Mike took a sideways glance at Beth, and as expected, her tears were flowing freely. He tried to swallow the hard lump in his throat, but only succeeded in making himself feel sick.

Morgana turned to a table at her side, and picked up a jug and a hammer.

"As this vessel is made from earthly clay and can be broken, so the vessels of our souls too are eventually broken and returned to our Mother Earth. As the vessel is broken, so our souls are free to continue their journeys unhindered."

Morgana struck the jug with the hammer and allowed the pieces to fall at her feet.

"Estreya's spirit is free and has begun her journey to the Summerland. She will always remain in the hearts that have loved her, unfettered, unbroken, and beautiful. Blessed Be."

The response went up from the crowd, "Blessed Be."

It wasn't over, and Mike was finding it increasingly

difficult to retain his composure.

Morgana continued, "The dark of night gives way to another bright day, so too, our sorrow gives way to joy. Grieve awhile, but then put away your tears, knowing that the wheel ever turns, and so it is, that in the Summerland, there will be reunion with those who have gone before us.

"Our rite is now ended, and now is the time to celebrate our part in the life of Estreya. Merry Meet, and Merry Part, and Merry Meet Again."

Morgana nodded to the two Druids who lowered their flaming torches to the base of the pyre, and in seconds it was consumed in flame.

That was it - his emotions tipped over the edge, Mike turned away to allow his tears. Pendragon he may be, but he was human, and in his own world he was simply, Mike Travis, and he was allowed to cry.

Merlin was at his side then. "Something in your eye, Pendragon?"

"Hell, yes. Sorry, it was too much, just too bloody much."

"Yes, Morgana has a way of bringing forth emotions. I expect that you aren't up to a repeat performance?"

Mike frowned. "How do you mean?"

"Nimue."

"Nimue is going to have the same honours?" He was sincerely shocked.

"I know that in your world they used to bury sorcerers at the crossroads with a dead dog or something, but this is Avalon. All deaths are honoured. Nimue may have lost her way, but she was a daughter of Avalon and she will be given the respect of one at her passing."

"*Lost her way?* But it was you that killed her!" Mike was incredulous.

"Pendragon, you have much to learn of our ways. Nimue will already be learning her mistakes. We must allow her that. Morgana is tired and is going to rest after we have done the right thing by Nimue. After she is rested she plans to take your daughter to the stone circle and perform the ritual that will contain her powers until such time as they can develop at a natural pace. Your wife may attend but you, Pendragon, are not invited. The ritual is a highly sacred one where women only are permitted."

"So, I'm supposed to sit and twiddle my thumbs!"

"I am not familiar with that pastime, but I highly recommend you accompany me on one of mine."

"Which is?"

"The consumption of a large quantity of alcoholic beverage."

Mike threw back his head and laughed aloud. "In my world we call it getting pissed."

"Indeed. I shall expect you later at the Meeting House. In your world, I believe you call it 'The Pub'."

"You know what, Merlin? I believe that I will accompany you to Nimue's ceremony. I am beginning to understand."

Merlin nodded his approval. "Of course you are. You are Pendragon."

Nimue's service was no less emotional, but was unattended except for Morgana and the two Druids, Merlin and Mike. When it was over, Morgana retreated to the quiet of her house, with only Ayleth for company. Already she loved the girl, and would do her best to allow her to grow into the woman that Estreya had been. There could be no more fitting a tribute.

Mike had kissed Beth on the forehead as she had cradled the exhausted, and now sleeping, Adain. She had readily agreed to Merlin's suggestion, but warned Mike to stop short of the vomiting phase.

Mike had grinned at her and made no promises, and went in search of Jack, Jim and Ben as confederates in crime. After all, he reasoned, this was Jim's stag night. A custom of his world of which he believed Merlin would approve.

CHAPTER THIRTY THREE: AND A WEDDING

Mike never knew, and Beth would never tell him, what had taken place within the stone circle. And that was the way it should be, he thought. There had to be some things that were sacred. Women's things. What he did know, was that he had a monumental headache, and the birds that were usually twittering in the apple trees, were conspiring against him in a cacophony of noise that threatened to split his skull open.

He tried again, without much success, to open his eyes to the glaring sunshine. He remembered then - it was Jim and Rowan's wedding day, or in their parlance, their Handfasting. And he was to be Avalon's equivalent of Jim's Best Man. His stomach did a somersault, and he closed his eyes as the room in which they had spent the night did a three sixty degree turn at hyper speed.

He turned gingerly to where Beth should have been, seeking a modicum of sympathy. Her half of the bed was empty. He groaned.

Some vile denizen of the depths of Hell, opened his door and allowed the bright morning sun to fall on his face. A pain pierced his brain with the force of a red hot needle shot from a pistol. He groaned again.

"Morning!" chirped the denizen, whose voice had an uncanny resemblance to Jack.

Mike swore, colourfully and with unaccustomed flare.

Jack approached with caution; he remembered only too well from the previous night that Mike's stomach was volatile in the face of alcoholic assault. His shoes bore the proof.

Mike cautiously opened his eyes. Jack was standing by

the side of the bed, grinning like an idiot on speed. He had a small clay goblet in his hand, which he proffered dangerously close to Mike's nose.

"Here, drink this. Rowan sent it over." He sniffed at it. "Doesn't smell so bad, and she said it will have you right as rain in no time. Personally, I think I'd prefer a bowl of thick porridge but hey, when in Rome!"

The visualisation of a bowl of thick porridge was enough to earn Jack a description that cast doubt on his parentage. Jack was the kind of git that could drink a lake of alcohol dry and still rise like a lark in the morning with a sense of well-being that would impress the Dalai Lama.

After several minutes of muddled thought, Mike's brain processed the idea that he couldn't feel any worse, so he took the goblet and downed it in one.

He felt its progress through the various apertures and tubes of his anatomy, and only moments later began to feel less like something the cat had eaten and vomited onto the carpet.

He flexed his neck. No pain. He turned his head. The room remained stationery. He opened his eyes. No red hot needle.

"Whatever that is, I want it bottled."

"Come on, get up," replied Jack. "Jim's looking for you, there's a wedding in an hour and he kinda needs his Best Man. Here." He handed Mike two rings. "He gave me these to give to you and said if you lose them, you'll be better off dead." Jack laughed, and surprisingly, it didn't sound like the banging of a thousand dustbin lids in Mike's head. He tried a smile. With no ill-effects, Mike tried to progress to a small laugh. There could be no dispute. Rowan was a witch.

"Where's Beth and Addie?"

"Over in Rowan's gaff. Women only again, I'm afraid. But I think you'll be glad of that. Did you know that Rowan has chosen Adain to walk with her as her flower girl thingy? Sweet, eh?"

"Jack, I have a limited attention span so please, spare me details. It's probably better if Beth doesn't catch sight of me like this."

"Too late mate, you had the roasting of a pig on a spit when you fell through the door last night. I think we could safely say that she wasn't impressed."

"Oh, shit."

"Yeah, well, it's a wedding. What can I say? It has a strange effect on women. I think you'll probably get away with it. Now come on! Jim threatened something unpleasant to a delicate part of me if I didn't get you over there in ten minutes. You're gonna love your outfit."

Mike crossed his eyes, his imagination in overdrive.

He glanced at the chair at the side of the bed, on which was laid a pair of breeches, and a silk tunic. Not so bad. A reminder of his hippy phase. He could do that. In fact, he was beginning to think he could do anything. Damn, the contents of that goblet were impressive. He made a mental note to ask Rowan for the recipe.

There was little for him to do for Jim by the time he finally arrived at his room. But Jim was on cloud nine, and a late Best Man wasn't going to spoil anything.

They made their way to the Sacred Well.

Everyone was there, from the eldest druid to the youngest maiden. Morgana was now garbed in golden silk and she stood at the wellhead ready to witness the sacred rite. Mike scanned the faces and couldn't see Beth. Jim noticed his concern.

"She's with Rowan and the Maidens. Adain is to be her Sacred Maiden. I guess Beth is with her until they get here. Relax, will you. It's me that's getting married."

Morgana beckoned to them and they walked to the edge of the well. Someone began to pluck at the stings of a harp and everyone's chatter ceased.

Mike turned around in time to see Beth slip into the crowd and Rowan enter the sacred ground.

She was serene in a flowing gown of silver silk which

enhanced her olive skin and red hair, so typical of the faerie race. Adain spotted Mike and smiled shyly. She wasn't aware of what was happening, but she had a woman's instinct for romance and centre stage.

Rowan reached Jim and handed her posy of wild flowers to one of the Maidens. She lifted her head and spoke the words that opened the ceremony.

"May this place be sacred to The Goddess and The Horned God as we stand here together to be joined in the Rite of Handfasting."

Jim replied, "So must it be."

Rowan continued, "May the Beings of Air be with us and tie the bonds between us, closely."

Jim said, "May the Beings of Fire bring passion to our union."

Rowan smiled at him, the dazzling smile of the bride on her wedding day. "May the beings of Water bring the depth of the oceans and the purity of the mountain spring to our love."

Jim took her hand. "May the Beings of Earth bring stability to our love."

Together they said, "May the Goddess and the Horned God bless our union."

Rowan spoke again. "All Goddesses are one Goddess and the wise call her 'Woman'. She is the creator and she brings desire to the father, the Horned One."

Jim was beaming now and word perfect. "Let me look in the face of this woman and see in her the Goddess in all her phases, all her beauty, and all her love."

There was a pause and then Rowan said, "Jim, will you take me, to your hand and your heart, as your bride and comforter in this life and those to come?"

"I will. Rowan, will you take me to you hand and your heart as your husband and protector in this life and those to come?"

"I will."

Jim nodded to Mike indicating that this was the time

for him to relinquish the rings, faerie-made and blessed. He obliged and they exchanged them in silence.

Morgana stepped forwards then and they placed the palms of their left hands together, and she bound them together with white ribbon.

Rowan was radiant as she said, "I give you my hand, my heart and my spirit at the setting of the sun, the rising of the stars and in the name of The Goddess, now and for all lives and times. Death will not part us, for we shall be born again and meet and know and love again."

Mike knew, without looking, that Beth would be awash with tears. Jim continued, "I give you my hand, my heart and my spirit, at the setting of the sun and the rising of the stars and in the name of The Horned God now and for all lives and times. Death will not part us, for we shall be born again, and meet and know, and love again."

Morgana reached forward to their hands and cut the white ribbon with a golden knife.

One of the older priestesses brought forwards a broom and placed it in front of the couple, who jumped over it, wreathed in smiles.

A cheer went up from the gathering.

The ceremony was over and everyone made their way to the Meeting House. Mike caught Beth's warning glance and he shrugged at her with a boyish grin. He was forgiven.

CHAPTER THIRTY FOUR: THE LADY OF THE LAKE

Amidst the merry making and quaffing of copious amounts of mead and wine, Merlin and Morgana sought Mike out.

Merlin looked serious. "Pendragon. There is something you must do before leaving us."

"If it doesn't involve the processional path up the Tor, I'm in."

Morgana's look quelled his joking.

"What can I do?"

"As you know, Excalibur cannot live in the outer world. Before you leave, you must cast it back into the lake. There it will remain with the Lady of the Lake until you have need of it, and come to reclaim it again."

"But I thought that Nimue was the Lady of the Lake."

"There will always be a Lady of the Lake, just as there will always be a Lady of Avalon. One has been chosen, and she dwells beneath the waters ready to receive Excalibur. Come."

Mike glanced at Beth, who was happily exchanging baby stories with other young mothers. He smiled to himself. All was as it should be. He followed Merlin and Morgana to the edge of a small lake, where Merlin handed him Excalibur with reverence.

Immediately Mike felt the power surge as he lifted the sword. It was heavy, weighed down with its own magic and power. A golden light grew quickly from the tip of the blade to the hilt, making it glow with an inner fire. He felt that power in his hands, his arms, his entire being and, in the seconds that followed, his brain downloaded the secrets of the ages. The magick was his now. He felt it,

209

knew it, and sensed it in every fragment of his soul. The world could be his to command.

He blanked out the thought and took a deep and shuddering breath. He raised the sword high above his head, marvelling at the light that sparkled on the previously dull water.

Without thought, he flung Excalibur through the air in a blinding arc of light. It sailed through the air, cutting through the veil. He watched, breathless as from the dark water a hand emerged, followed by a slender arm. The elegant hand reached up to meet the falling sword and grasped it by the hilt, before it made contact with the lake.

The water boiled and churned as both arm and sword disappeared beneath the surface of the lake. And he felt its loss.

Morgana sensed his emptiness. "In Avalon you will always be honoured as the Pendragon, but in your world it will be as a dream, for how else can you live in two worlds and keep your mind? But you will always find your way through the mists and return to us in a time of need. Yours or ours. And when your daughter becomes a woman she shall come to us for training as a priestess. And when the Great Mother calls to me, and I hear her ravens, she will become Adain, the Lady of Avalon.

Merlin laid a hand on his shoulder and said, "Enough blood has stained that blade, but now its power lies in the hands of a good man, and for now it rests with the Lady of the Lake. Come, Pendragon, it is time for you to return to your world."

Jim and Rowan were waiting to say their farewells at the landing stage. The barge was making its way through the mists and Mike could feel the call of home.

The day would come when Avalon would return. But that day was not yet. For now it was enough that it had moved closer.

In the silence of the barge, Mike contemplated his friends. Jack, more like a brother, and Ben, the biker who had been a psychiatrist, a priest and an exorcist. He looked on Beth and Adain, and he knew that he was a rich man.

Ben sensed his gaze.

Mike said slowly, "You know what, Ben? I think you have to be the strangest priest there is."

Ben grinned back at him. "Na. I think that honour goes to Father Paul Beckett."

Mike put his head on one side and looked for more.

Ben grinned. "He's a vampire," he said.

Mike nodded. Of course he was. "Let's go home," he said.

THANK YOU!

To my Reader:

Many thanks for buying *The Merlin Manuscript*, I hope you enjoyed reading it.

If you did enjoy it, please post a review at Amazon, Goodreads or your favourite social network site and let your friends know about *The Merlin Manuscript*.

I hope that this has whetted your appetite to read the other novels in the Mike Travis paranormal investigation series. You can find details of these in the next few page as well as the short stories collection: *Beginnings*.

Happy Reading!
All the best
Jan

ALSO BY JAN MCDONALD

BEGINNINGS

MIKE TRAVIS
PARANORMAL INVESTIGATIONS

MIKE TRAVIS
PARANORMAL INVESTIGATOR

BROOKSTONE COTTAGE, BROOKSTONE,
MONMOUTH, S. WALES

JAN McDONALD

BEGINNINGS

A bonus of five short stories for fans of the Mike Travis paranormal investigations

It all began for Mike Travis with a helicopter crash in war-torn Afghanistan that resulted in his being declared clinically dead; before expert combat medics brought him back to life.

But he came back with a gift. He could see ghosts.

These five short stories bridge the gap between what happened in the immediate aftermath of the crash to his arrival in Crowsmoor, Cornwall, where his help has been summoned in an effort to prevent the return of an ancient evil.

Beginnings charts his progress from his first encounter with a ghost to his becoming a recognised investigator into all things paranormal. For readers of the series, these five short stories will be familiar territory.

If you have a smartphone, you can buy Beginnings at Amazon by scanning the barcode below:

THE CROWSMOOR CURSE

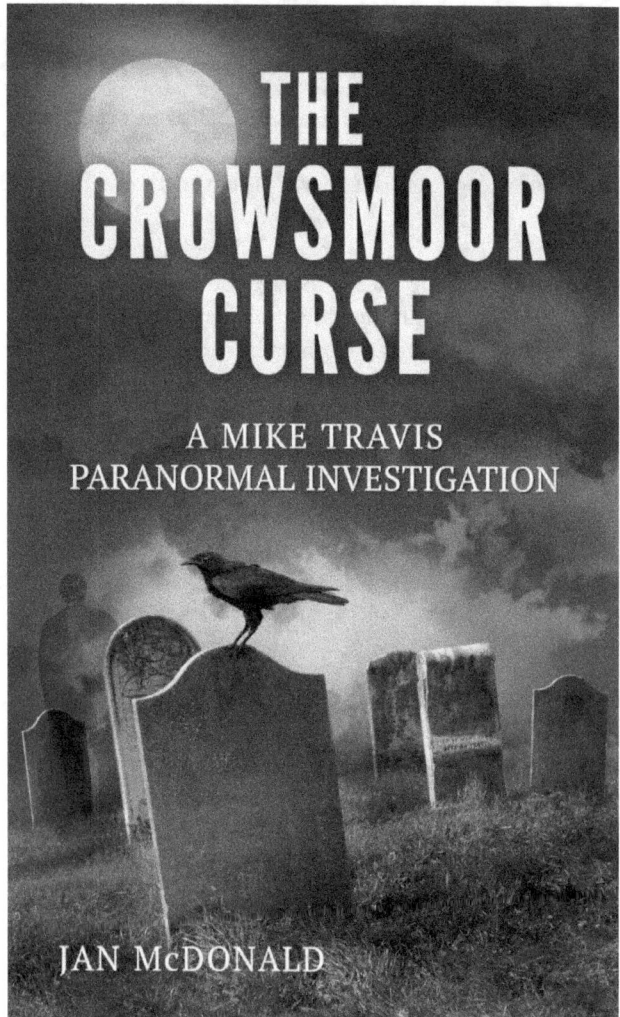

THE
CROWSMOOR
CURSE

A MIKE TRAVIS
PARANORMAL INVESTIGATION

JAN McDONALD

THE CROWSMOOR CURSE

The dead of Crowsmoor are light sleepers.

Some say they sleep with one eye open, keeping watch over the restless ones.

When Beth Trevithick is sent as parish priest to the isolated and scattered community of Crowsmoor, in the middle of bleak Bodmin Moor, Cornwall, she finds a community entrenched in fear and superstition and belief in an ancient curse born of dark magic.

She gets unexpected help in the form of Mike Travis, ex RAF helicopter pilot medically discharged after crashing in war torn Afghanistan, he has turned to his other love, the paranormal, devoting all of his time to paranormal investigation.

Beth soon discovers the fear and superstition in Crowsmoor are well founded and together with Mike fights for her own sanity and her life.

If you have a smartphone, you can buy The Crowsmoor Curse at Amazon by scanning the barcode below:

LONG SHADOWS

A MIKE TRAVIS
PARANORMAL INVESTIGATION

JAN MCDONALD

LONG SHADOWS

When Mike Travis and his pregnant wife Beth relocate to an idyllic cottage in rural Monmouthshire, they didn't bargain for a sitting tenant. The spirit of Adain Powell, brutally murdered by the lecherous and ruthless Judge Llewellyn in 1654, still haunts the cottage and adjoining wood, unable to rest until the truth surrounding her death and the wrongful accusation of her husband for her murder are brought to light.

In the cellar of The Black Mountain Inn, another is stirring. Judge Thomas Llewellyn's grave is unearthed and his old bones, his very old bones are the focus of black magic ritual intending to bring about his return.
It is soon more than Mike and Beth's new home that is at stake; it is their lives and the life of their unborn daughter.
Long Shadows is a story of both ancient and present day evil: to be read with the lights on.

If you have a smartphone, you can buy Long Shadows at Amazon by scanning the barcode below:

THE
SACRED
ARK

A MIKE TRAVIS
PARANORMAL INVESTIGATION

JAN MCDONALD

THE SACRED ARK

A longer pause and then a lowered tone.
"Jesus Christ, Josh. What have you found?"
An even longer pause.
"The Ark of the Covenant."

When paranormal investigator Mike Travis answers a call for help, he doesn't anticipate being flung headlong into Ancient Egyptian secrets in *The Sacred Ark*. An old acquaintance needs his help in his search for proof that his controversial theories are correct, theories which have resulted in him being ridiculed by the world of archaeology.

Mike finds himself in the heart of the Sinai desert pursued by government and Vatican hit men, all desperate to find the same thing, the Ark of the Covenant. What secrets does it hide and where will it take him?

If you have a smartphone, you can buy The Sacred Ark at Amazon by scanning the barcode below:

I have read the diary from cover to cover and now I wonder if there is an element of reality in what she has written and that in fact the truth is more terrifying than anything she could imagine.
I have enclosed her diary so that you can decide for yourself whether or not there is something happening that would explain her situation and perhaps even find some small way to help her. I am sure that somewhere inside her is the mother that I once knew.

When Mike Travis stays at home to finish writing his next book he doesn't expect to be embroiled in a new case.
A mysterious letter and diary are sent to him and he soon finds himself battling ancient demons with the help of friends old and new.
He believes that Victoria Little is the victim of possession rather than mental illness and sets out to free her and rid her of the vicious demon Ahriman. The fight takes him into the world of ancient dark magic which has stretched its legacy into lives past and present.
Who is connected to this ancient evil and which side of the Abyss do they live on? Who can he trust?

A treat for fans of paranormal horror and suspense. You won't want to put this down though you may at times wish you could!

If you have a smartphone, you can buy The Haunted Diary of Victoria Little at Amazon by scanning the barcode below:

MIDNIGHT WINE

JAN MCDONALD

MIDNIGHT WINE

Ex Catholic priest, Beckett, is out for blood. Vampire blood.

History is repeating itself and Beckett enlists the help of Dr Lane Dearing, herself a powerful vampire, in an effort to save the beautiful Katerini from a sadistic and vicious Undead. Their struggle leads them from the mysterious mountains of the Brecon Beacons in Wales to an isolated monastery in rural Greece where they encounter one of the Ancient Ones who has his own reasons for wanting Katerini.

Midnight Wine is a vampire tale of love, revenge and sacrifice. Vampires are real. They exist.

And they are out there...

If you have a smartphone, you can buy Midnight Wine at Amazon by scanning the barcode below:

LYCAN

FROM THE AUTHOR OF
MIDNIGHT WINE

LYCAN

JAN MCDONALD

LYCAN

Acceptance didn't sit well with ex-Catholic priest Beckett.
And being a vampire wasn't going to come easy. Struggling
with his new life he finds himself helping another whose
life has been dramatically changed. Jude Mason is suffering
from Post Traumatic Stress Disorder; but Beckett and the
elegant vampire Lane Dearing believe that there is more to
it.
Much more.
Their efforts to understand and help the man are
hampered by unfinished business. In the tiny monastery in
Greece, where they believed they had ended the killing
spree of ruthless and savage vampires, one has survived.
They must return to finish what began years previously
with the death of the beautiful newly turned vampire,
Katerini.
In Greece, there is as much to lose as to be won and with
the stakes high someone has to pay the price.

*If you have a smartphone, you can buy Lycan at Amazon by
scanning the barcode below:*

CONTACT DETAILS

Visit the authors website:
jan-mcdonald.co.uk

Follow on Twitter:
www.twitter.com/janmcdonald1

Cover designed by: Raven Crest Books
Cover photography © Andrey Kiselev - Fotolia.com

Published by: Raven Crest Books
www.ravencrestbooks.com

Follow us on Twitter:
www.twitter.com/lyons_dave